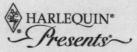

In Harlequin Presents books seduction and passion are
always guaranteed, and this month is no exception!
You'll love what we have to offer you this April....

Favorite author Helen Bianchin brings us
The Marriage Possession, where a devilishly
handsome millionaire demands his pregnant
mistress marry him. In part two of Sharon Kendrick's
enticingly exotic THE DESERT PRINCES trilogy,
The Sheikh's Unwilling Wife, the son of a powerful
desert ruler is determined to make his estranged wife
resume her position by his side.

If you love passionate Mediterranean men, then these
books will definitely be ones to look out for! In
Lynne Graham's *The Italian's Inexperienced Mistress*,
an Italian tycoon finds that one night with an innocent
English girl just isn't enough! Then in Kate Walker's
Sicilian Husband, Blackmailed Bride, a sinfully
gorgeous Sicilian vows to reclaim his wife in his bed.
In *At the Greek Boss's Bidding*, Jane Porter brings you
an arrogant Greek billionaire whose temporary blindness
leads to an intense relationship with his nurse.

And for all of you who want to be whisked away by
a rich man... *The Secret Baby Bargain*
by Melanie Milburne tells the story of a ruthless
multimillionaire returning to take his ex-fiancée
as his wife. In *The Millionaire's Runaway Bride*
by Catherine George, the electric attraction between
a vulnerable PA and her wealthy ex proves
too tempting to resist.

Finally, we have a brand-new author for you!
In Abby Green's *Chosen as the Frenchman's Bride* a tall,
bronzed Frenchman takes an innocent virgin as his wife.
Be sure to look out for more from Abby very soon!

The Desert Princes
by Sharon Kendrick

Proud and passionate…
Three billionaires are soon to discover the
truth of their ancestry.

Wild and untamed...
They are all heirs to the throne of the desert
kingdom of Kharastan.

Though royalty is their destiny, these sheikhs
are as untamed as their homeland!

From the magnificent Blue Palace to the wild
plains of the desert, you'll be swept away
as three sheikh princes find their brides.

Coming soon:

May 2007
The Desert King's Virgin Bride

Sharon Kendrick

THE SHEIKH'S UNWILLING WIFE

The Desert Princes

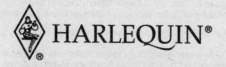

HARLEQUIN®

TORONTO • NEW YORK • LONDON
AMSTERDAM • PARIS • SYDNEY • HAMBURG
STOCKHOLM • ATHENS • TOKYO • MILAN • MADRID
PRAGUE • WARSAW • BUDAPEST • AUCKLAND

ISBN-13: 978-0-373-12620-0
ISBN-10:   0-373-12620-4

THE SHEIKH'S UNWILLING WIFE

First North American Publication 2007.

Copyright © 2007 by Sharon Kendrick.

This edition published by arrangement with Harlequin Books S.A.

® and TM are trademarks of the publisher. Trademarks indicated with
® are registered in the United States Patent and Trademark Office, the
Canadian Trade Marks Office and in other countries.

www.eHarlequin.com

Printed in U.S.A.

All about the author...
Sharon Kendrick

When I was told off as a child for making up stories, little did I know that one day I'd earn my living by writing them!

To the horror of my parents I left school at sixteen and had a bewildering variety of jobs: a London DJ (in the now-trendy Primrose Hill!), a decorator and a singer. After that I became a cook, a photographer and, eventually, a nurse. I waitressed in the south of France and drove an ambulance in Australia. I saw lots of beautiful sights, but could never settle down. Everywhere I went I felt like a square peg—until one day I started writing again and then everything just fell into place.

Today I have the best job in the world: writing passionate romances for Harlequin. I like writing stories that are sexy and fast-paced, yet packed full of emotion—stories that readers will identify with and that will make them laugh and cry.

My interests are many and varied: chocolate, music, fresh flowers, bubble baths, films, cooking and trying to keep my home from looking as if someone's burgled it! Simple pleasures—you can't beat them!

I live in Winchester and regularly visit London and Paris. Oh, and I love hearing from my readers all over the world...so I think it's over to you!

With warmest wishes,

Sharon Kendrick
www.sharonkendrick.com

To Andy Thompson, dear friend—
who reminds me of cool cathedral squares
and almond croissants!

CHAPTER ONE

YOU didn't have to be drowning for your life to flash before you. Nor to be sleeping to feel you had stumbled into a nightmare.

And this was her worst.

Alexa blinked her eyes rapidly, like someone emerging from the water—their vision blurred so that they couldn't see clearly—and found herself thinking that maybe it wasn't him. For a split second a fragment of optimism floated before her as she narrowed her eyes to watch the man who sauntered with such careless grace down the cobblestoned street. But hope died as he grew closer and she saw a group of women stop talking mid-sentence and turn their heads to follow his path.

He walked like the leader he undoubtedly was—a man born to money, as well as having made more than enough of his own. Tall and striking, he had crisp dark curls, hard black eyes and a proud and haughty look on a face which in repose looked faintly cruel.

His olive skin was dark—even for a Southern Italian—and a shamelessly exotic air had only added to his mystique in his native city of Naples. Glamorous mother; father unknown.

He was wearing a perfectly cut pale grey suit over a lean, hard body, and as he walked the women watching him almost melted on the spot. It would almost have been comic if it hadn't made Alexa's heart ache with a pain which should have disappeared a long time ago and yet deep, deep down was a feeling far more acute than pain.

Fear.

She licked her lips. Giovanni.

Giovanni—her husband.

Jealous, possessive, unrealistic, idealistic. Giovanni…

Silently she said the name she had tried to forget but never would—for how could she, when she was still tied to him by law, unresolved feelings and by something deeper still? Something so precious that if…if…

Alexa swallowed. Had he seen her? Her heart skipped a beat as that stupid hope flared into life once more. Did he know she was here?

But even before she met the ebony glitter of his eyes, training themselves on the shop window like a hunter's gun, or watched him beginning to cross the road towards the building, she knew that it was a dumb question to ask.

Of *course* he knew she was here. Why else would the black-hearted millionaire be wandering down a quiet English road instead of swanning around his hot and noisy Naples in that sleek little sports car he used to drive, with all the men shouting Gio! and the girls smiling and swaying their hips as he passed?

What else did he know? Had he…*found out*?

Oh, please. The world began to blur again, and she clutched the flimsy piece of silk she was holding. Please don't let him know.

Skin icing and heart beginning to pound, Alexa could feel the palms of her hands growing damp, and she put down the silk T-shirt she had been folding with shaking fingers. No wealthy customer would part with cash for an over-priced item if it was covered in splodges of her sweat. She licked her dry lips, telling herself it was insanity to try to second-guess the situation. Just see what he has to say and play it cool—surely you can do that, considering what's at stake?

The shop door pinged, and she looked straight at him as he walked in, fixing a smile to her lips which she hoped was just the right mixture of formal politeness and mild curiosity. The kind of smile that any estranged wife would give to a husband who had given the dictionary a new definition for 'unreasonable behaviour'.

'H-hello, Giovanni,' she said, but she heard her voice tremble, and he heard it too, for she saw the black eyes briefly narrow as he tried to interpret its origin. 'This is a—'

'What?' he questioned, deadly as a snake.

'Surprise.' She swallowed, feeling her throat constrict on the word.

'Ah! Such understatement, *cara mia*!' he murmured 'Did you really expect to go through the rest of your life without ever seeing me again?'

'I hadn't really given it much thought.'

'I don't believe you,' he said softly, and his eyes

flicked her a mocking look. Not think about him? The moon would fail to rise in the heavens before that should happen! 'All women who have known me are obsessed with me—and in many ways you have known me better than most, for you are the only woman I ever married.'

But Giovanni knew that it had been more than just the legal tie of their marriage which made her knowledge of so unique—a marriage which had been far stronger and less easy to shrug off than he had anticipated. It was because Alexa had seen him with his guard down—she had witnessed Giovanni veering towards the vulnerable—and she had taught him a lesson that he should have known all along: women were never to be trusted.

Alexa's fixed smile became a grotesque kind of grimace. 'Did you…did you want to speak to me?'

Jet-black brows were raised in arrogant query. 'The alternative being that I want you to sell me some women's clothes—perhaps shopping here for one of my mistresses? What do you think?'

If only he knew! If only he had an inkling about the crazed thoughts which were swirling around in her mind like an out-of-control whirlwind. *Because you know that what you have done to this man is wrong?*

She willed the voice of her conscience to cease— dampening down its clamour with a reminder of the harsh and bitter words he had spoken to her. *Everything she had done, she had done for a reason.* 'I can't talk now. I'm working.'

'So I see.' He glanced around the shop's interior, af- fecting interest—but in reality it was to allow the beating of his heart to steady. He was taken aback by its thunderous pounding—for he had underestimated her impact on his senses. Or maybe he had simply forgotten.

Hungrily, he let his eyes feast on her. Her bright hair was caught back in one of those severe French plaits you rarely saw these days, and she was wearing a black pencil skirt and white blouse—presumably some kind of uniform for working. Yet it didn't look anything like a uniform when she was wearing it. With the slim skirt skimming the gentle curve of her hips and the silky shirt caressing the swell of her breasts, she looked like a favourite male fantasy—buttoned-up, yet red-hot and hungry underneath. Giovanni swallowed. Later.

'Still a shop assistant?' he questioned sardonically. 'Isn't this where you came in—unless you own the place, of course?'

'No, I don't own it.'

So there had been no sudden change in her fortunes. No lover to lavish his wealth on her, having been reeled in with that unique blend of supposedly innocent sensuality. Those pale green eyes which could range from serene to feisty and a hundred expressions in between. She had the kind of body you wanted to cover in diamonds—and then slowly remove them, one by one.

Had it surprised him that she had not approached him for a hefty divorce settlement? He supposed it had—but maybe her lawyers had advised her that a mere three-month marriage would not yield much in the way of alimony.

'Hardly what you'd call rapid promotion, is it?' he

mused. 'Shop assistant in some small backwater of a place you grew up in.'

How effortlessly fluent was his English—and how brutally accurate was his contempt for her situation! Alexa gave him a non-committal smile. 'Well, we can't all be captains of industry,' she said quietly. 'Listen, Giovanni—no one was ever going to be in any doubt that you were the achiever in our relationship, but I really *don't* have time to stand around and chat.' Especially about something as painful and as potentially explosive as their past.

He glanced around the empty shop. 'But you don't have any customers!' he observed caustically. 'If this were my place then I'd give it a dramatic overhaul.'

'Well, fortunately for me, it isn't. So what is it that you want, Giovanni?' She blinked up at him, wondering if he could hear the slight crack of pain in her voice—because sometimes emotions just crept up on you, whether you liked it or not.

What if he had come to tell her that he wanted his freedom? That he had met someone new and fallen in love—only this time it was the real thing, not some youthful cocktail of lust and unrealistic expectations. 'You can tell me quickly.'

Giovanni heard the note of hope in her voice and gave a slow smile. 'You think I've travelled from Italy to *tell you quickly*?' he echoed silkily.

He had her senses spinning and she wanted it to stop. She wanted the rapid hammering of her heart and the feeling of faintness to pass, along with the regret and all the other things he had stirred up inside her within the space of a few minutes.

Alexa drew a deep breath. 'You should have warned me you were coming,' she said, in a low voice. And how would she have reacted if he had? Run away until she was certain the coast was clear, taking Paolo with her? But you couldn't keep running away all your life. Suddenly, an intimation of terror began to whisper its way over her skin. 'You should have warned me,' she repeated, more urgently now.

Giovanni looked at her trembling lips. Not for a moment had he thought she might have grown immune to him—but Alexa's reaction was *very* interesting.

She was edgier than he might have expected in the circumstances. And why was that? he wondered. Because she'd realised what she had thrown away? Or because she wanted him to take her into his arms and kiss her—to press his hard heat against the pliant softness of her body and drive his throbbing hardness deep inside her until she begged for release?

Giovanni's sensual lips curved into a cruel smile as he felt the rush of heat to his groin and the powerful beat of anticipation—yet he experienced slight dismay, too and the faint prickle of anger, because the feelings she provoked in him defied all logic.

Memories of betrayal and deceit washed over him when he looked at the pale oval of her face, and yet there was lust, too—a fierce sexual hunger which he had never completely satisfied. Surely that must account for the sudden strange lurching of his heart?

The agenda which had brought him here today was simple: the invitation burning a hole in his pocket and a desire that his wife accede to his wishes. And yet there had been curiosity, too. A sense of something never quite completed, nor put to rest—a question that everyone whose marriage had failed must ask: *what if?*

Giovanni's mouth hardened. But that was pure unnecessary sentiment—and he was not a man given to sentiment. Putting that aside, he knew what he really wanted, and it was more than her agreement to accompany him on such an important occasion. Ah, *si*. He intended to have her one last time. He would feast on her body and take his fill from it—and then… He swallowed. Then that last lingering legacy from their ill-fated marriage would be satisfied and he could move on.

Inside the luxurious interior of the store, the lights shone down and transformed her hair into pure spun gold. Yet the light played tricks just as the heart did, for her hair was not really gold, but a strange colour somewhere between red and gold—the colour they called strawberry-blonde. Such a rare shade to adorn a head, and especially so in his native Southern Italy.

Her eyes were the fresh colour of pistachio and her skin looked like creamy vanilla. The first time he'd met her he had told her she looked like an ice cream sundae, and only just stopped himself from adding that he wanted to lick her all over. Much later he had teased her that he wanted to dip his spoon in her—and her corresponding blush had sealed her fate. His face darkened.

She was his.

Alexa.

Alexa O'Sullivan. A name as unusual as her hair, as her soft curving body, pale with silken skin. She looked as innocent now as she had done on the day they had met. But innocents did not lie, nor did they cheat.

He was prepared for the anger, but unprepared for the regret. That he had ever married her in the first place? Or that he had let her pale green eyes and berry-coloured lips lull him into believing a fantasy?

'What time do you finish?' he said softly.

For a moment Alexa hesitated, recognising that he wasn't going to go away until he'd got what he came for, no matter how much she wanted him to. The most sensible thing would be to arrange to meet him for lunch the next day—which would give her time to compose herself, prepare herself for any verbal battle. But that would mean him hanging around—maybe even staying in one of the local hotels—and then what? Giovanni asking questions—smarming his way into the confidence of adoring women staff, or—worse—local people beginning to look closely at his stunningly dark Mediterranean looks and putting two and two together.

'I finish at six,' she said quickly.

'Good. Good.' Giovanni's black eyes glittered with satisfaction. The first part of his mission was accomplished—the second would be to decide where to take her. A hotel? With the convenience of a bedroom within walking distance? Why not start as he meant to go on? Hunger curved the edges of his mouth into a hard smile. 'I'll pick you up here.'

'No!' The word flew out before she could stop it, but Alexa wanted neutral territory—a bland, safe environment. Though was anywhere really safe with Giovanni? Didn't the power of his presence subtly dominate his surroundings, so that no matter where you were all you were aware of was him? She met his questioning stare. 'My boss doesn't like anyone else in the shop while I'm emptying the till,' she babbled. 'I have to look after the takings.'

'I shouldn't think there'll be much in the way of *takings*, judging by the lack of customers,' he observed sardonically, raising his eyebrows. 'You will have to do better than that for an excuse, *cara*.'

It was arrogant of him to suppose that she *needed* an excuse not to talk to him—but then, his arrogance had never been in question. 'I won't be able to concentrate if you're breathing down my neck.'

He smiled. Better. Much better. 'No, I can see that might be a problem,' he agreed evenly. 'So, where shall I see you?'

Alexa's mind was racing. She would have to phone the childminder, of course, and arrange a later pick-up, but that should be okay.

She ran through all the possible venues to come up with the one where she was least likely to know anyone—but as a woman who rarely went out in the evenings she had a pretty big field to choose from. 'Meet me in the Billowing Sail,' she said. 'Just after six. It's a little pub, tucked away in the corner of the harbour.'

'A pub?' he echoed.

'That's right.'

'But I don't like pubs, Alexa,' he said softly. 'You know that.'

And *she* didn't like being forced into a meeting with a man who could still turn her emotions upside down. He—like she—would just have to put up with it. 'I'm afraid that pubs are part of English life—and none of the coffee shops will be open at six.'

'Then let's have dinner instead.'

'D-dinner?'

'The meal that people eat in the evenings,' he enlightened her sarcastically. 'You know.'

Alexa felt her heart slam nervously against her ribcage. One thing she knew for sure—no way could she endure the forced intimacy of a restaurant, with its subdued lighting and leisurely service.

She shook her head. 'No—not dinner.'

His black eyes narrowed. 'You mean you don't want dinner, you don't eat dinner—or you're having it with somebody else?'

For a second she was tempted to say yes—that the man of her dreams would be waiting at home for her, with a warm smile and an even warmer bed. Because most men would give up and go away if they thought she'd moved on and found herself another man. But Giovanni wasn't most men, and his jealousy was legendary. It had helped destroy their relationship with its warped, dark poison—and Alexa didn't think she could face seeing it activated now.

She shook her head. 'No, I'm not having dinner with someone else. But I'm tired,' she said truthfully. 'It's been a long week, and I don't imagine we're going to have a lot to say to each other—certainly not enough to fill a whole meal-time. A quick drink should do it.'

For a minute their eyes met in a silent battle of wills, and he thought about trying to impose his on her—but wouldn't that put her defences up? Alexa had something he wanted, and so for now he would play this her way. And besides, he would soon talk her out of her dismissive suggestion—or maybe kiss her out of it. His heart began to race in anticipation. *A quick drink*, indeed!

'Very well,' he agreed. 'I will see you in there, soon after six. *Ciao, bella.*' And he turned his back on her and walked towards the door, seeming to take all the light and the colour with him as it shut behind him with a little pinging of the bell.

In a daze, Alexa watched him go, her knees feeling as if they were about to give way, scarcely able to believe that what she had most dreaded had just taken place.

Only it isn't over yet. Not by a long way.

She turned round and reached for the box of tissues she kept beneath the counter, for customers to wipe off their lipstick before they slithered into costly items of clothing, and dabbed furiously at the tears which couldn't seem to stop welling at the corners of her eyes. She didn't even register that the shop door had opened again, and it wasn't until she heard a voice behind her that she whirled round and saw her boss standing there—an elegant blonde in her fifties, a concerned look on her face.

'Teri!' she gasped. 'I was miles away. I didn't—'

'I know you didn't. That was your husband, wasn't

it?' guessed Teri perceptively. 'The Italian Stallion currently wowing the female population of Lymingham?'

Alexa nodded, trying to compose herself. 'Ex-husband,' she corrected, swallowing back the tears.

'I didn't think you were divorced?'

'We're not—officially—but divorce is just a piece of paper,' said Alexa fiercely. 'Just like marriage.'

'You think so?' questioned Teri wryly, and then a note of curiosity crept into her voice. 'How come we've never seen him before?'

Alexa tensed. 'Because he lives in Naples and I live here, and we don't have a shared life together.'

'That's not what I mean, Lex,' said Teri gently. 'He's Paolo's father, isn't he?'

There was a pause. It was just as Alexa had thought—the resemblance was as unmissable as a dark cloud suddenly obscuring the sun. The boy was a carbon copy of the man. 'Yes,' she whispered.

Teri's eyes narrowed in a slowly dawning comprehension, and she raised the tips of her fingers to her mouth. 'And he doesn't know, does he?'

There was a terrible silence.

'No.'

'Oh, Alexa.'

But Alexa shook her head, remembering Giovanni's bitter words. The torture of living with him once he'd decided she didn't measure up to his exacting standards of what a woman should be. The accusation he had flung at her as she had left his house and his city and his life. And she remembered his immense wealth and determination. Oh, no. She would be a fool to start having some kind of euphoric recall about the man she had married—and an even bigger one to underestimate his power.

'He would take him away from me if he knew,' she said flatly. 'And that's the truth.'

'But how…*why?*' asked Teri in confusion. 'I mean, how on earth has all this happened?'

How, indeed? Why did some people's dreams get smashed to pieces while others merely faded away like the end of a film?

She could tell Teri that she had travelled to Naples and fallen in love with that vibrant, chaotic city which was flanked by Mount Vesuvius, the island of Capri and the crystal-blue waters of the Tyrrhenian Sea. Just as she had fallen in love with Giovanni—or *thought* she had. With his dark good looks and dangerous charm and his determination to possess her—yes, *possess* her—who could have resisted him?

Fresh out of university, and undecided about a future which had seemed to have a gaping hole in it since her mother had remarried and emigrated, Alexa had gone to Italy to brush up on a language at which she was already passably fluent.

It hadn't taken her long to decide that Italian men were after one thing—easy, uncomplicated sex with women who were prepared to offer it to them on a plate. And Alexa hadn't been. Her one foray into matters sensual had been enough to make her cautious—because the man to whom she had lost her virginity had

had all the sensitivity of bull. But then she'd met Giovanni, and all her best intentions had flown out of the window.

Working in the air-conditioned splendour of the city's biggest and plushest department store, Alexa had become a bit of a novelty. A foreigner who spoke cool and fluent Italian—and there certainly weren't many English shop assistants in Naples! Customers had been charmed by her accent, and men in particular had come to purchase soft leather gloves from the pale-skinned creature with the green eyes and red-blonde hair and the pale, poised air. Sales had increased. She'd been given a raise and moved onto handbags.

And then one morning Giovanni had walked in, and everything had changed. In an instant she had become the victim of the feeling which had swamped over her— a feeling she'd never really believed in until it happened to her. But then no one ever did.

The world had stopped spinning, became suspended and frozen—and everything in it had blurred into insignificance except for the man who had sauntered in, seemingly oblivious of all the eyes upon him as he homed in on her like a moth to the flame. And Alexa had fallen in love.

She had not known that he owned the store, and several like it throughout Italy, or that he featured on all the Best-Dressed and Most Eligible lists—usually somewhere near the top. All she'd known was that he had eyes like ebony and skin which seemed especially dark—like sleek, polished wood—and that the suit he wore did little to conceal the hard, honed perfection of his body. Her mouth had dried, but she'd hidden it behind her polite shop assistant's smile.

'So, you are the woman who is causing all the excitement,' he murmured.

Alexa glanced around the shop, taking deliberate note of all the women who were watching him, and she smiled as she answered him in Italian. 'And you are the man who seems to be doing just the same!'

He was slightly taken back—as much by her retort as by her fluency. Giovanni had been told that she spoke his language, but he had not expected it to be so...so... perfect. 'I have been told that you are very beautiful,' he said huskily. 'But words do not do you justice. I have never seen a mouth so begging to be kissed.'

Alexa's eyes became shuttered. Because these were the kind of glib phrases she knew were meaningless. In the past weeks she had become a dab hand at spurning the advances of amorous men—though it had never seemed remotely difficult before. 'Are you interested in buying a handbag, sir?'

Giovanni thought of a hundred ways he could react to her question. He could say yes, go through a flirtatious little pantomime of asking her advice and then buying the one she liked best—probably the most expensive one— and presenting it to her with a theatrical flourish before asking her out for dinner. But some cool reserve in the pale green eyes told him that this strategy would not get him the result he wanted. She was not flirting with him, he realised with a certain astonishment. *Not flirting with him*!

'No, I am not interested in handbags. I am interested in showing you Naples.'

'I have a map.'

'And I have a car.'

Alexa glimmered him a smile. 'I like to walk. But thank you all the same.'

'I am used to getting my own way,' he purred.

'Then I have a feeling that this time you're going to be disappointed.'

'I am never disappointed when I set my heart on something.'

Alexa discovered that he was rich, and that he changed his women more often than his cars. She told herself that the best thing would be to avoid him—but Giovanni da Verrazzano laid siege to her, and the more she refused his invitations, the more ardent became his pursuit.

If she'd had been older and more experienced she would have realised that her unwillingness to go out with him was only increasing his determination, and his admiration. But she wasn't doing it to play games. She was doing it because she was frightened of being hurt.

So that by the time she could refuse him no longer, and agreed to have a chaste lunch in a tiny restaurant scented with jasmine and overlooking the city, Giovanni had placed her on a pedestal as high as Vesuvius itself.

He swept her off her feet with a masterful arrogance which left her reeling—and yet it was his surprisingly tender restraint which ensnared her and fuelled the fires of a passion she hadn't known she possessed. The almost reverential respect he showed for her determination not to fall into his bed meant that Alexa could relax.

For the first time in his life Giovanni listened to a woman, and talked with her—and it was a novel experience. She made him laugh—while he showed her that a sexy and virile man could have the soul of a poet.

He fell in love—was blown away by it—as innocent as a child beneath the onslaught of this powerful feeling. The cynical man of the world who had seen and done everything was as susceptible as the next when it came to the age-old vulnerability of the heart.

But nobody told them about brevity of the *colpo di fulmine*—the thunderbolt of love—which crashed into lives for such a brief moment before crashing out again. If anyone had tried, they'd have never believed them.

'Marry me,' he said one day.

Alexa's heart lurched, and threatened to deafen her with its sudden wild pounding.

'But—'

'Marry me, Lex,' he said again—softly, sweetly—his lips brushing over hers in way which made her want to faint with pleasure.

Maybe it was madness, but in Giovanni Alexa saw her glorious future. He wanted to take care of her. Her beautiful, strong, old-fashioned Italian seemed to be the answer to something she hadn't even been aware she was looking for.

So they married, in a ceremony which was intended to be simple—until Giovanni's mother arrived back from a spending spree in Monte Carlo to turn it into

something of a spectacle. But nothing could destroy
Alexa's slightly disbelieving pleasure in the unexpected
twist her life had taken. It felt like a dream—it *was* a
dream, she thought happily, forgetting that dreams
didn't stand up to the cold light of day.

And hers crumbled on their wedding night itself,
when Giovanni made the discovery that his bright-
haired and perfect bride was no virgin. He stilled,
staring down at her in disbelief, words torn from his lips
moments after he entered her.

'There has been another?'

It was a question designed to break the bubble of her
passion—though for a moment Alexa wasn't quite sure
she had heard properly. But then he repeated it—or rather,
he shouted it—and the lovemaking which up until the
moment of penetration had been like her wildest expectations come true—suddenly mushroomed into something else entirely. Something ugly. Something shameful.
Giovanni's face closed up—closing her out—but he didn't
stop what he was doing. He carried on moving inside her,
and the only chink in his armour came in that brief
moment when he lost control and cried out her name.

Afterwards, she lay back against the pillows, feeling
as if he had ripped something from her heart and her
soul, staring up in the moon-washed silence as his terse
and furious interrogation began.

And the first night of their honeymoon was only the
start of it—for his discovery had awakened the dark
green serpent of a jealousy which up until that moment
had lain dormant. Every move she made was watched;

every statement she uttered was analysed. She had slept with five men, no—ten. Or was it more than that? And how many was she sleeping with now, other than him? She must tell him, for he needed to know!

Yet he seemed determined to give her satisfaction—almost as if he was demonstrating a master-class in sex. As if he wanted to show her how good it could be. And in some ways it was. In his arms, Alexa gasped out her pleasure time and time again, but the lack of emotion and the simmering anger on Giovanni's face made her feel empty afterwards. Like a beach, when the tide had turned and flowed away.

It was a slow kind of torture, and Alexa lasted only three months of her doomed marriage. Then she had fled vowing never to revisit that black landscape of despair ever again—but she would never forget Giovanni's snarled and angry words ringing in her ears.

At least we must give thanks that you aren't pregnant—for how would we ever know the identity of the father?

Yes, the facts were simple—it was what lay behind them which was complex. She had been too young to know the difference between love and lust, or between protection and possession. She should have known something about Italian men—and Southern Italian men in particular—before she committed herself to marriage.

'Are you going to tell him?' asked Teri now, her concerned voice bringing Alexa back to the present. 'That he has a son?'

Alexa wiped away the last tear and shook her head. 'I can't,' she said, swallowing defiantly. 'I can't afford to.'

CHAPTER TWO

AFTER Teri had left the shop, Alexa forced herself to deal with practicalities. She phoned the childminder, who said that, yes, of course Paolo could have his tea there.

'I'll pick him up at about seven-thirty,' said Alexa, in a voice which suddenly sounded shaky. 'Will you…will you send him my love?' She heard the emotion trembling in her voice as the childminder said she would, and that they would see her later.

Alexa put the phone down. Her proud and beautiful little son would not be happy to have his normal routine changed, but he would soon have the childminder acceding to his every wish just by looking at her from beneath the thick curtain of his dark lashes and twisting her with that heartbreaking smile.

What would Paolo say if he knew that his daddy was in town? She bit her lip with pain and guilt—but it was pointless allowing her mind to go there. Hadn't she gone over this, over and over again, and decided this was the only way that her son could be guaranteed a life that wasn't filled with acrimony and trauma?

But by the time Alexa finally locked the shop door at the end of the day she was a bag of nerves, and knew she had to pull herself together. It was pointless trying to predict what she would say or how she would behave until she knew the reason why Giovanni had suddenly turned up here today. And if she walked into the pub looking like a shivering wreck, then his suspicions would only be alerted.

Changing out of her working clothes, she pulled on jeans, sweater and jacket, and stared back at her image, knowing that she was dressed in a way which was practical and smart rather than feminine. But appearances mattered—particularly to a man like her husband. He would judge her by what she was wearing and she would not, *not* be found wanting. So she brushed her hair and added a touch of lipstick, and rubbed her finger against her cheeks in an attempt to put some colour there.

At least the crisp breeze which blew in from the sea took her breath away and made her feel properly alive— even if her heart felt dead. She walked along to the harbour, where little boats bobbed in the water with their masts chattering and where seagulls cawed in their relentless search for food.

On such a cold evening there were few people hanging around, and it seemed so desolated and so very English that for a moment Alexa could scarcely believe that her estranged husband was sitting waiting for her—here, in this little town. Her territory, she thought. Not his.

The pub sign creaked, and Alexa hugged her coat

tightly to her as she dipped her head to walk into the warm, beamed interior and look around for Giovanni.

He wasn't hard to find. The pub was fairly quiet, with just a few office workers having a quiet pint before setting off home for the familiar evening routine, and Giovanni looked overwhelmingly exotic in comparison.

On a table in front of him stood two glasses of red wine, and his long, muscular legs were stretched out in front of him—pulling the material tight over his groin and unashamedly accentuating his masculinity.

Alexa thought how deeply olive his skin looked beneath the soft lighting—yet it gave off a soft golden radiance which contrasted with his thick hair, as black as the coal which lay waiting to be thrown onto the roaring fire.

And suddenly she felt a terrible yearning—like someone standing in an icy waste who had just sighted a thick cashmere blanket. For how long was it since she had looked on a man and felt anything approaching desire?

Not since Italy.

And she had never desired anyone the way she had Giovanni—how could she? Who could possibly follow a role model like him?

Well, she wasn't going to think of that now. Keep focussed. Find out why he's here and keep it simple. Pinning a smile to her lips, she began to walk towards him.

Giovanni's eyes narrowed as he saw her, and again that alien and unexpected feeling wrenched at him. How pale her face looked, he thought with a frown. And how did she always manage to project that image of being all alone in the world—so that a man wanted to reach out and safeguard her? His frown deepened. Because that was the game she played—one that all clever and beautiful women engaged in. His own mother had excelled at it. Alexa was simply capitalising on her assets—emphasising her strange fragility and her pale, doe-like beauty.

Forcing himself to concentrate instead on the darkened bow of her mouth, the sway of her hips, and the thought of her breasts hidden beneath the bulky jacket, he was rewarded with a familiar leap in his groin. He rose to his feet as she approached, because his manners were always impeccable, even if the dark light flashing from his eyes was anything but conventionally polite.

'Here I am,' she said flatly.

'So I see.'

They stared at one another like two new boxers in the ring, who were trying to psych the other one out.

He would never have allowed her to go out wearing such a bulky, waterproof jacket as the one which now sparkled beneath fine droplets of seawater, he thought. Yet the dilemma with someone who looked like Alexa was that on the one hand you wanted her to display that magnificent body of hers—while on the other you did not want other men seeing it. But they were separated now, and none of the normal rules counted. How she dressed was nothing to do with him, for he was interested only in seeing her without any clothes on at all.

His eyes flickered over her, to where her glorious

hair tumbled down in windswept strands over her breasts. 'At least you've let your hair down,' he observed softly.

'Giovanni, we aren't here to...'

'To what, *cara*?' he questioned innocently.

'To—to make personal remarks like that.' To make her feel like a real woman for the first time in years and remind her of his consummate skill as a lover. And wasn't she in danger of regarding even *that* through rose-tinted spectacles? She must force herself to remember the reality of their wedding night and its bitter conclusion. 'It isn't appropriate,' she finished.

Giovanni heard the slightly despairing note of appeal in her voice and bit back his smile. This was good. What was it that the English said? He was *getting under her skin*. Just as she had once got under his, playing disingenuous games in order to hook him, as women had been attempting to do since he'd first started shaving.

'Sit down,' he said, his eyes narrowing at her look of genuine hesitation.

'I don't know if I should.'

His mouth curved into a mocking line. Did she really imagine that he would let her walk away from him a second time?

'I said, sit down,' he repeated silkily.

Come to think of it, she wasn't sure she could walk straight out again—even if he'd told her she could. The feelings which had surged over her since he'd entered the shop suddenly took their toll, and with legs which were suddenly weak Alexa sank down onto one of the overstuffed leather sofas, glancing around her as nervously as if she was a woman on a blind date.

Sometimes when she was out she felt self-conscious, or paranoid as if people were staring at her. But today they really were. And it was nothing to do with a windswept woman on her way home from work—but everything to do with the exotic man who had just sat down opposite her. He was lounging back in his chair like a dangerous, undiscovered species who needed a warning notice attached to him.

He pushed a glass of wine towards her. 'You look as if you could use it.'

Alexa took the drink but didn't touch it. Just looked straight into his eyes and willed herself not to respond to all those potent signals he was sending out. But most potent of all was the heartbreaking similarity between him and Paolo. The same thick forest of black lashes, and the slash of high, slanting cheekbones. The same dark curls—though Paolo's were more of an ebony tumble and Giovanni's had been expertly clipped to lovingly define the proud shape of his head. She shook the thoughts away.

'How did you find me?' she questioned, curling her fingers around the glass, as if doing that would warm their frozen stiffness.

'Oh, finding you was simple, *cara*—far easier than I expected.' He shrugged. He had been surprised she was still here—but then, didn't women always go back to somewhere they'd known? She had lived here before she had come out to Italy. Before her mother had moved off to live in the wilds of Canada, and before he had foolishly decided that Alexa needed looking after and had married her.

His mouth hardened. 'I tried your old phone number and got your voice on the answer-machine.'

'And if you hadn't?'

He shrugged, but his eyes glittered. 'Then I should have had to employ someone to find you. Anything is possible.'

'A...detective?'

'Something like that.'

'But you didn't? Get a detective, I mean?' she questioned, until she saw his face and realised that she'd said too much. Underestimated his razor-sharp intelligence. He must surely have noticed her wide-eyed fear and be questioning its source. So better start back-tracking before it was too late.

'Whatever is the matter, Alexa? Anyone would think you had something to *hide* from me.'

'Oh, don't be so melodramatic!' she said brightly, though inside she hated herself for the unspoken lie which fell from her lips. 'I'm just fascinated to find out what has brought you here.'

'Are you?' He traced his forefinger along his bottom lip thoughtfully. Of course she was going to be jumpy— what woman wouldn't be, in her situation? Was she looking at him now and realising what a stupid mistake she had made? But *she* was the one who had to live with the consequences of her own stupidity—and that was not the reason he was here.

'Yes, in truth it is a fascinating story,' he agreed, but for once in his life the words did not come easily—there was no template for this kind of situation. He ran his finger around the rim of his wine glass and realised that although they were separated he was still treating her like a wife. For simply by marrying they had forged a deep bond he had experienced with no other woman— no matter what had happened between them subsequently. Why else would he be about to confide in her an incredible story he had told no other? 'You remember my mother?' he asked suddenly.

It was not the opening Alexa had been expecting, and it took her off guard. 'Yes, of course I remember her,' she answered slowly. 'She's a pretty unforgettable character.' Natala—his glamorous, gorgeous mother, with her penchant for diamonds and those slinky black satin dresses which were as tight as a second skin. Until Alexa had met Natala she hadn't realised that mothers could look like film stars.

'How is she?' she questioned, not quite sure of the etiquette in asking after a woman who had once been overheard pronouncing her as—'*ordinary*. And she has no *money*, Gio!'

His lashes came down, concealing all but a dark gleam of light in his eyes. 'She died last year,' he said bluntly.

Alexa gasped, everything else forgotten—because his mother had been relatively young. 'Oh, Giovanni— I'm so sorry,' she said instinctively, and only just stopped herself from leaning forward to touch him.

Giovanni's eyes narrowed and she saw in them the

brief chink of pain. But then it was gone—clicked out—
like the shutter of a camera.

'Did you come here just to tell me that?' she questioned uncertainly.

His black eyes hardened. 'No. Of course not.'

There was a pause as he seemed to search for the right
words. It was so uncharacteristic of Giovanni to hesitate
that Alexa felt herself stiffening with apprehension.

'What, then?' she said nervously, because precious
minutes were ticking away—and it wasn't just that she
wanted to be back on time for Paolo and not to alienate
the childminder by taking advantage. She also wanted
to be away from the still-powerful sexual pull her
husband exerted—away from the foolishness in her
heart which made her want to put her arms around him
and draw him close in a gesture of comfort.

He tapped his long olive fingers against the polished
surface of the table. 'After she died I was going through
her papers and I made a discovery.'

'What…kind of discovery?'

Sifting and sorting through the files of information
in his mind, Giovanni began for the first time to place
them in some kind of coherent order. 'The unwelcome
kind—that informs you that you have been labouring
under an illusion for most of your life,' he said, and his
voice sounded suddenly harsh.

'What *illusion*?'

His voice hardened. 'As you are aware, I grew up believing that my father was a Spanish aristocrat—one
who refused to publicly acknowledge me, even though

he was prepared to pay generously for my upkeep and my mother's jewels. My mother told me that her silence about his identity to the rest of the world would guarantee her a lifetime's riches. And it did.' The stony expression in his eyes matched the sentiment at the heart of his words. 'She also led me to believe that he had died—and I had no reason to distrust her.'

'You mean she was lying?'

Giovanni threw her a look of mockery. 'Why? Would you feel an affinity with her if you knew that to be the case?' he questioned acidly.

'I'm not interested in raking up old scores, Giovanni,' she answered quietly. 'What are you trying to say?'

'That my father is not Spanish at all—and he is not dead. Though he is very old, nearing the end of his life, and—'

'And?' she prompted, on a whisper.

'I am the son of a sheikh,' he said at last, aware even to his own ears—how bizarre his words must sound. He could see his own reaction mirrored in her widened eyes.

'What?'

'My father is a sheikh.' But through the haze of unreality bubbled a feeling of intense...*satisfaction*. It was as if he had found the missing bit of himself—which, in a way, was exactly what had happened. 'More specifically, he is Sheikh Zahir of Kharastan,' he added. And then, as if to lessen the emotional impact of his words, he raised his jet brows in question, as if he were a university professor quizzing a student. 'You have heard of it, perhaps?'

For a moment Alexa forgot their history, forgot her own dark secret and her fear of the man she had married—because his startling piece of information wiped all other thoughts completely from her mind. She didn't even stop to question it—Giovanni wouldn't lie about something like that. Why on earth would he? He had the riches and the power that most men hungered for—he wouldn't invent royal blood unless it were true. And wouldn't that just make him a million times more attractive to the opposite sex? she thought, with a sudden pang of wistfulness.

'Of course I've heard of it,' she breathed. 'The papers have been talking of nothing else for weeks. There's a big royal wedding taking place there soon, isn't there?'

She tried to remember a bit more, but she had mainly looked at photos of the handsome groom and his beautiful fiancée while she'd been sitting in the hairdressers. What with working full-time, looking after her son and running a home some things had to give—and reading the foreign news section of the papers was unfortunately one of them. Alexa frowned. 'But I thought it was the Sheikh's *son* who is getting married. And isn't he half-*French*?'

Giovanni gave a grim smile, for in a way she had made this easier for him. 'Yes. He is. The Frenchman's name is Xavier,' he said. 'And he is—as you say—the Sheikh's son. He is also my half-brother.'

'You mean there's more than one son? I...don't understand, Giovanni.'

Hadn't he thought exactly the same thing himself,

when the incredible facts had first been presented to him
by the Sheikh's aide—the man they called Malik? For
in one swoop Giovanni had gone from being a man with
no family to finding himself a father and a half-brother.

'Although he had a long marriage, it seems that the
Sheikh had two illegitimate offspring who were born in
Europe during that time. Xavier was one and I am the
other,' he explained slowly. 'Neither of us was acknowledged publicly, for fear of offending the Sheikh's wife, but
after her death it was his dearest wish to be reconciled with
both sons, and for them to meet each other.' Giovanni's
face was implacable. 'And that is what has happened.'

'You mean—you've met them?'

Giovanni nodded, his black eyes brilliant -seeking,
restless, almost yearning. As if starting out on this bizarre
quest had wakened some kind of dormant wanderlust in
his blood. As a man who—apart from his one ill-fated
experience with Alexa—was used to encasing his
feelings in ice, it was strangely unsettling to feel this way.

'*Si*,' he said, his voice now rough with a passion he
had not expected to feel for any country other than his
Italian homeland. 'I have met them. I flew to Kharastan.
To a palace which is bluer than the brightest sky of high
summer. To a land where falcons dominate the stark
desert and hunger waits around every corner for the
unwary. And there I was introduced to my…' He toyed
with the word *family* as a cat might play with a mouse
before striking. But Giovanni did not strike. His lips
curved, for the intimate title seemed inappropriate for
a couple of men he barely knew—no matter what their

blood-tie was. 'I met the Sheikh and Xavier,' he said carefully. 'And the woman Xavier is to marry. They want me to go to their wedding.'

There was a pause while Alexa tried to digest the incredible facts he had told her. In any other circumstances she might have flung her arms around his neck and told him she was happy for him. Or she might have delved deep into his mind and asked him how he felt about suddenly discovering that he had a ready-made family?

But Alexa could not afford to do any of those things—even if their relationship had been the kind which would allow it. They had parted bitterly—with too much said which could never be unsaid. And there was too much at stake for her to risk asking him anything other than the time of his flight back to Italy.

'It's a very interesting story,' she said carefully, and put her glass down on the table. 'But I don't understand why you've come all the way from Italy to tell me about it when we're...'

'When we're what, Lex?' he prompted softly. 'Neither married, nor divorced? What is it that you say in England—neither fish nor fowl?'

'We're separated. Estranged.'

'But still legally bound—so in theory we are still family. Why is that, I wonder? Why did you not file for divorce, *cara*?' he questioned softly. 'Did some clever lawyer advise you to bide your time—telling you that *il tempo viene per chi sa aspettare*?'

'All things come to those who wait?' Alexa translated slowly, for her command of the language had grown

rusty. She hadn't used it for years. Hadn't wanted to—
just the sound of it took her back to a place too hurtful
to reside in.

'*Bravo, bella*,' he applauded softly. 'Yet—while you
may go to the top of the class—you have avoided answering my question. *Have* you been advised by a
divorce lawyer? Closely watching my business dealings
and then slowly closing in to make the maximum financial kill?'

Alexa felt the rapid skitter of her pulse, sensed a
sudden and unknown danger. 'You're a cynic, Giovanni.'

'Maybe life made me that way—and still you avoid
my question.'

Because if she answered him then the whole story of
Paolo would come tumbling out. Yet she could not avoid
divorce for ever, could she? She'd somehow imagined
that Giovanni would file for divorce early on after their
split, and that whole subject would come up within the
sanctity of a legal framework. Protected by lawyers,
she would have been safe. But now too much time had
elapsed—and that created its own problems. She
honestly couldn't see a way out of the maze she had
helped create.

How could she tell him the truth when it was so
blurred in her mind and in her heart that she wasn't really
sure any more about what was real and what was not?

*And if you show him any weakness he will pounce on
it.*

'I saw no reason in filing for divorce.'

'Not even for the settlement?'

Alexa hesitated. She could have done with a settlement. But pride had stopped her. She had chosen independence and freedom from his obsessive jealousy over all else—so in the circumstances could hardly ask him for any money. If she did that then the truth would come out, and the chance of a generous settlement was too high a price to pay if it meant that Giovanni could wrench Paolo away from her.

'Perhaps you wish to remain married to me?' His black eyes were gleaming as he continued with his relentless line of enquiry. 'Maybe you regret that the division of our relationship ever occurred? Did you walk out thinking that there might be a million other men like me out there, only to discover just how wrong you could be?'

Alexa opened her mouth to question his arrogance—to remind him of his unrealistic expectations of her which could never be fulfilled. But not only were accusations and recriminations futile, they also had the potential to be dangerous. Because was there the tiniest intimation of truth behind them? Just go. Get up and go.

'There's no point in making inflammatory remarks, Giovanni.' She bent down to retrieve her handbag, repressing a sigh of relief that her ordeal was almost over. Yet there was some part of the feminine psyche—and hers in particular—that made her experience a terrible, tearing pang at the thought that this really might be the last time she saw him. And part of her was longing to ask him a stream of questions about his discovery. But it's none of your business, she reminded herself. He's not part of your life.

Isn't he?

The goading question inside her head disturbed her more than it should have done, and Alexa gripped the strap of her handbag as if her life depended on it. 'If that's everything you wanted to say, then I really must be on my way. It really was…' She shrugged a little helplessly. 'Fascinating.'

'Do not be absurd, Alexa,' he warned silkily. 'You can't just get up and leave.'

'I can do anything I please,' she returned. Because now the hammer of fear was beginning to strike at her heart—until she reminded herself that not even Giovanni would dare to keep her there by force. 'That's the joy of being single!'

Stung to anger, she had given away the fact that there was no man on the scene—but Giovanni did not feel it necessary to allow himself a quiet smile of satisfaction. Even if she's had a lover he would soon have been dispatched—for who on earth would ever win a woman over Giovanni da Verrazzano?

'You still haven't heard the reason why I have come here today, Alexa—surely you are a little bit curious?'

She feigned uninterest but suddenly her senses prickled. There was an air of thinly veiled excitement about him. And something else too—something she couldn't put her finger on.

Was *he* going to ask for a divorce? she wondered, and to her astonishment felt her heart plummet like a coin dropped from the top of a tall building. Wasn't it strange how something as sensible and as irrevocable as the legal termination of a long-dead marriage should have the power to hurt, even after all this time? 'Okay, I'm curious. Tell me.'

He smiled. 'I want you to accompany me to Kharastan. I want you at my side for the wedding of my half-brother.'

CHAPTER THREE

ALEXA stared at Giovanni, her heart now beating very fast.

'You want *what*?' she echoed incredulously, as if somehow she might have misheard him—though in reality every silk-dipped word had been as clear as the look of enjoyment on his dark, rugged face. He was getting a kick out of this, she thought.

'Stop playing for time, Alexa—it really is very simple. Come with me to Kharastan,' he murmured, and his eyes narrowed in sardonic query. 'You can afford to be so blasé about it?' he mused. 'I confess myself surprised—after all, it isn't every day that a woman gets an invitation to a royal wedding. Doesn't the prospect of that tempt you?'

She guessed that there were women who would have been thrilled to bits by the prospect of such a high-status event—no matter what the price they had to pay to get there. But Alexa wasn't the kind of woman who could be swayed or seduced by money or trappings. Hadn't she left every item of clothing and jewellery behind in Naples when she had fled the marriage?

'You have to be out of your mind!' she choked. 'Give me one good reason why I should accompany you *anywhere*?'

'Because you are my wife.'

'In name only.

'In name is enough.'

'Not for me, it isn't.'

'But I am talking about *my* needs, *cara*—not yours.'

Alexa picked up her wine glass and managed to successfully negotiate a mouthful of wine before putting it tremblingly back down on the table. She felt it burning its way down to her stomach, but at least it gave her a little bit of courage.

'You're not making sense, Giovanni—and even if you were the answer would be the same. It's no. How could it possibly be anything else, in the circumstances?' She could see that stony, obdurate look she knew so well on his face. 'There must be women who would queue up around the block to accompany you!'

He stilled, and when he spoke his voice was as cold as ice. 'You would not care? It does not bother you to think of me taking another woman?'

She injected bravado into her voice. 'Why should it?'

So she *did* have the calculating heart of a woman who could just walk away from a marriage without a backward glance or single regret. Hadn't there been some small and crazy part of him which thought she might *react*—that she might have *cared*?

Giovanni's face darkened with a rage which made him want to hurt her. 'It does not concern you to think of me kissing her? Nor to imagine me deep inside her body, with her legs wrapped tight around my back, until she cries out her pleasure?'

Unprepared for his sexual taunt, Alexa was not expecting the hot swell of nausea which rose up within her. She flinched. 'Giovanni—'

His mouth curved and he made no attempt to hide the triumph which washed over him in a heady wave. 'Of course it does!' he gloated. 'You would have to be made out of stone for it not to affect you.'

And nobody could accuse her of that. Her body had been soft and warm. It had trembled violently beneath his touch as if he'd been a virtuoso playing a brand-new instrument. Where he had led, she had been content to follow—he had drawn up the boundaries of their sexual relationship and she had seemed happy to comply with them. When she had nodded in flushed agreement to his stern suggestion that they wait until after the wedding before they consummated their relationship, he had known a thrill of expectant pride like no other.

He had been searching for innocence, and Alexa had led him to believe that he had found it. Not until their wedding night had Giovanni discovered what a sham it all was, and by then it had been too late to do anything about her deceit. Other than to despise her for making a fool out of him. And Giovanni had never been made to feel a fool before.

Something in his heart had died on their wedding night. Yet through his hurt and his anger Giovanni had been determined to take the pleasure he deemed rightfully his—and he had taken delight in coaxing from Alexa her own reluctant response. She had known that he despised her for what she had done and yet she had been unable to resist him. For her, every time she'd sobbed out her orgasm it had been a kind of defeat; for him, a kind of victory.

'Admit it,' he urged softly. 'You do not like the thought of me lying with another woman!'

Of course she didn't like it—it made her feel violently sick. She swallowed down the bitter taste in her throat and hoped her face didn't reflect her inner turmoil.

'Just as *I* do not like the thought of you lying with another man,' he breathed.

So nothing has changed there, thought Alexa. 'This is ridiculous,' she said, clasping her hands together and resting them on the table in front of him as if in silent appeal—like a handcuffed prisoner in the dock. 'We're separated. We haven't seen each other for almost five years—one of us ought to get around to filing for divorce. It's not exactly a textbook description of an easy relationship—yet you turn up out of nowhere and ask me to go with you to this wedding? You can't honestly want that on such an important occasion.'

'Ah, but that is where you are wrong,' he contradicted. 'I want this very much. In fact, it is you I want and only you.'

For a moment Alexa wondered if her ears were playing tricks on her—for weren't those the very words she had once dreamed of Giovanni saying? Coming to her with a contrite and heartfelt declaration that he had been wrong to treat her like a *thing*. A possession. Someone he had seen as perfect, but not quite real. A woman who could only be judged by his own archaic standards. And what woman in the world could have lived up to them?

But of course he would not have changed. Men like Giovanni considered themselves always to be in the right—to admit otherwise would go against every arrogant atom of his alpha-male make-up.

'Well, you can't have me.'

Carefully he placed his palm over her clasped hands, covering them entirely with his warm skin, and he felt her start, saw the pistachio-green eyes darken and her lips part in unconscious invitation.

'Can't I?' he said softly.

For a moment Alexa let herself go there—to the place where sensation dominated everything else. The touch of his hand made her tightly locked fingers relax—unfurling as if they were sticks of ice thawing under the unexpected heat of a winter sun. Such a seemingly innocent contact, and yet it brought all those long-suppressed and forbidden feelings flooding back. Skin against skin. The sensation of being touched, stroked, cajoled. Entered. Pleasured.

'Why would you want to take me to the wedding with you?' she whispered.

Deliberately, he lifted up her hand, to let his thumb begin a slow, sensual circle around her palm. 'Because I want a lover while I am there—a sexual partner for the duration,' he murmured. 'And it will be less offensive to Kharastani sensibilities if that woman is my wife.'

There was a short, disbelieving pause.

'A sexual partner *for the duration*?' she bit out, as if he might suddenly turn round and say that he was sorry—he hadn't been thinking straight and hadn't meant to say it. But of course he didn't. His black eyes just glimmered with amusement, and Alexa realised that he was actually *enjoying* himself. 'Are you out of your mind?'

She hadn't even noticed he was still holding her hand, he realised, and leaned a little closer. 'Let me be honest with you, Alexa, in a way you were never honest with me. We should never have married—I accept that. But there's still a lot of sex which didn't happen between us—I feel it and you feel it too. I can tell just by looking at you, by the way you tremble beneath my touch. So why fight it?' He gave a short laugh as he looked down at the fingers which were lying so compliantly cupped in his. 'I don't imagine you're ever going to get an invitation like this again.'

Snatching her hand away, Alexa shuddered and scrambled to her feet. There was, she realized, no diplomatic way to do this—there never had been, not with Giovanni. He would forge ahead until he got what he wanted. Only in this case he wasn't going to get it—and the sooner he realised that, the better.

'The answer is no,' she said in a low voice, fighting her instinct to shout it out—but she didn't want to draw any more attention to them. 'It's over, Giovanni. It should never have begun. Please—let's just leave it. We've said all there is to say. Except maybe goodbye.'

She walked out of the pub, her head held high and her cheeks burning—glad that her lifestyle meant she rarely ever went to places like this, and neither did her customers. At least it wasn't likely that she was going to run into anyone asking *Who was that gorgeous man we saw you with last night*?

But once outside she started running as if her life depended on it. She risked a quick glance over her shoulder, but thank God—oh, thank *God*—Giovanni hadn't followed her.

She was out of breath by the time she had reached the quiet cul-de-sac where Paolo's childminder lived, but at least she had begun to relax. Of course he wasn't going to follow her. He might want a 'sexual partner for the duration'—to use his own sickeningly cold-blooded choice of words—but he wasn't so desperate that he was going to start haranguing her to get her to agree to accompany him.

'Mamma!'

Paolo hurled himself straight into her arms the moment the neat little front door was opened, and Alexa's heart turned over the way it always did when she saw her handsome and clever little son.

But for once her joy was measured by other, uncomfortable emotions as she helped him into his duffel-coat.

Fear, yes—but guilt, too.

Because the huge brown eyes which gazed up at her so trustingly were so like Giovanni's? Was it seeing him for the first time in nearly five years which had made the similarities so apparent? Or was it the vague stir of her conscience which troubled her—a conscience she could usually manage to push away to the corners of her mind during the busy blur of everyday living?

'Where have you been, Mamma?' Paolo asked, his little hand firmly clasping hers as they walked up the narrow track leading to her tiny cottage.

'I went for a drink after work, darling.'

'Who with?'

'With…' What did she say? What could she possibly say? Oh, just with someone I knew a long time ago. Your father, actually. She felt her cheeks burning hot and red, but whether it was with guilt or shame at the heavy secret she carried, she couldn't be sure. *There was nothing else you could do—no alternative open to you—you would have lost your only child if you had tried!*
'Look, we're almost home, darling—shall I make us cocoa when we get in?'

'Oh, yes, *please*, Mamma!'

Alexa was so preoccupied with her swirling thoughts, and with opening the front door and switching on the light, that she didn't see the figure emerging from out of the shadows behind them, before it was too late.

Instinctively, she pushed Paolo inside—but that was probably a mistake, for the child stood in the full, illuminating glare of the light, staring up with fearless interest at the man whose powerful body almost filled the doorframe.

'Who are you?' her son asked innocently.

But Giovanni was staring at the child with a look of incredulity—frozen into astonishment by the sight of himself as boy—but the shock slowly left him, and he looked up and met Alexa's eyes.

A silent question was asked, and she nodded her head. For how could she do otherwise?

Yes, her eyes told him. *He is yours.*

'How old is your little boy?' he questioned, in a voice which somehow stayed steady. Because even though he knew the answer somewhere deep inside him, Giovanni was too much of an operator not to want to assemble all the facts before him. And it gave him time to think...

There was a pause. 'Paolo's four—and a quarter,' she said

Maybe he wouldn't believe her—why should he, when he had thrown all those accusations at her, his fevered and jealous mind imagining a whole catalogue of men she was supposed to have been intimate with? But five years on and he had changed, Alexa realised. Maybe it now suited him to see beyond the distortion of his own prejudices, or maybe he just could not deny the evidence of his own eyes—for she knew at the precise second when he accepted Paolo was his.

A brief shining moment of exultancy which was quickly replaced by a much darker emotion as he looked at her.

If she thought that she had seen bitterness there before then Alexa hadn't even come close to it—and now she almost recoiled from the vitriolic light which flooded over her in a dark blaze.

'Are you going to tell him?' he questioned softly. 'Or am I?'

CHAPTER FOUR

'TELL me what?' demanded Paolo.

Alexa bit her lip as she looked down at her son—at his beautiful, dark, oh-so-innocent face—recognising that once he was told his world would never be the same again. And shouldn't that be done with a little forethought?

She glanced up at Giovanni and his icy black gaze lanced through her like a sabre—but the recriminations which were bound to come her way were not important. Nothing was—except for Paolo. Deliberately she projected appeal from her eyes.

Please don't hurt him, went her silent message. *Hurt me, but please not him—for none of this mess is his fault.*

There was an almost imperceptible narrowing of Giovanni's eyes in response, a slight nodding of his dark head—or had Alexa imagined that?

'I am a friend of your mother's,' he said softly.

'I don't know you,' said Paolo stubbornly, and Alexa recognised that this strange man was stepping on the young boy's territory—or at least that was how Paolo was interpreting it. Would Giovanni be sensitive enough

to do the same? she wondered. 'I've never seen you
before. Are you Mamma's boyfriend?' he demanded,
with a suspicious scowl.

'Why, does *Mamma* have a lot of boyfriends?' questioned Giovanni, and sent Alexa a look of pure, shivering malice.

How could she stop this? He would never believe her
if she tried explaining that she'd never actually *had* a
boyfriend, because Giovanni took real delight in imagining the very worst about her.

'I knew Giovanni a long time ago,' said Alexa, in a
bright voice which sounded as if it was cracking open,
like a smashed nut.

The black eyes glittered with another *just-you-wait*
message.

Paolo nodded his dark curls energetically, the dark
eyes huge in his face as he stared up at the tall Italian.
'Are you staying?'

There was a tense silence, until Giovanni gave a soft
laugh which might have convinced Paolo that he had
found something amusing, but which failed to do the
same for Alexa.

'You'll have to ask your mother that,' he said, in a soft
voice which sounded like a threat.

'Look, we ought to shut the door—we're letting all
the warmth out,' said Alexa desperately, telling herself
that she must not go to pieces. She couldn't just
couldn't—not in front of her son. 'Giovanni—' This
time there was a new appeal in her face, a subtle but dig-
nified pleading in her voice. 'Why don't you come back

tomorrow? You could come for tea—you'd like that, wouldn't you, Pao—'

'I'm not going anywhere,' said Giovanni smoothly. 'As long as Paolo doesn't mind?'

Openly fascinated by such an exciting-looking man, and enchanted to be included in an adult decision, Paolo shook his head. 'Can you play games?' he questioned, tugging at Giovanni's dark cashmere overcoat.

'Just try me,' Giovanni murmured.

Alexa watched him follow Paolo into the sitting room with an expression which bordered on disbelief, wanting to pinch herself, to tell herself this wasn't happening, none of it—from the moment he'd strolled into the shop this afternoon, leaving a trial of emotional havoc in his wake to now. Hadn't she imagined there could be nothing as bad as his reappearance? How naïve could you possibly get? Because this was far worse— Giovanni discovering the truth in this way.

But there's a reason you didn't tell him!

It was imperative that she didn't forget that and stayed strong—because her strength was her only defence, and she needed every bit of it to protect Paolo.

Ignoring the hostility in his eyes, which bored into her whenever there was an opportunity during Paolo's sweet but unfair domination of the dice game they were playing, Alexa lit a couple of lamps and set about making up the fire. Only when there was a cheerful blaze crackling in the hearth did she venture into the cubby-sized kitchen to make the promised cocoa.

She couldn't imagine the sophisticated and urbane Giovanni sipping the milky, chocolatey drink—but she included a third mug, and some of the gingerbread men she'd made with her son, which were nearing the end of their life but were still just about edible. And Paolo would be so proud of them, she thought, as she slid them onto a plate—before pulling herself up short and slumping against the kitchen wall in horror.

What was she *thinking* about?

She wasn't thinking—that was the trouble. For a moment back then she had slipped into some kind of normal programmed response of a mother serving drinks to a guest. But she wasn't. This wasn't an exercise in Happy Families—not by any stretch of the imagination. Showing off Paolo's creative attempts at cookery was one thing—but that was as far as it went.

Except that she didn't have a clue what was going to happen next. Alexa wasn't stupid, and she had a measure of the man she was dealing with. The very last thing Giovanni da Verrazzano was going to do was jump back on a plane and disappear out of their lives again.

So what, then?

So she needed to have all her wits about her, that was what.

By the time she brought the tray into the sitting room the fire had really taken hold, and the whole room was lit with a crackling warmth. Firelight was not just for-giving—it was as flattering as candlelight. It flickered and danced and created all kinds of illusions, and it hid the shabby and rather ugly reality of the room—cloaking it instead with the golden-orange glimmer of flames. The cheap rented furniture glowed as deeply as any antique, and you didn't notice the rug was thread-bare beneath the glimmering light.

'Here we are!' said Alexa, her smile stretching so that she felt it might split her face, feeling as if she was performing in some horrible, cruel farce.

Two faces were raised to hers, so heartbreakingly similar—but while Giovanni's eyes glittered with un-ashamed enmity Paolo's were filled with love and trust.

Trust.

Would he still trust her after he had found out what was now screamingly inevitable? That he had a father. Why had she never stopped to think about that before?

Handing out drinks which nobody really wanted, she could see Paolo trying desperately not to yawn. And, although she was dreading the moment when she would be alone with Giovanni, Alexa knew that she couldn't put off her son's bedtime any longer. Scrambling to her feet, she held her arms out.

'Come on, sunshine—time for bed!'

But Paolo didn't leap up for a monkey cuddle, the way he usually did—instead he slid his hand into hers in a newly grown-up way which tore at her heartstrings and turned to look at Giovanni.

'Will you be coming back?' he questioned.

Giovanni nodded his dark head. 'Oh, yes,' he said. 'I'll be coming back.' And then, lightening his voice and his mood by a conscious effort of will, he dazzled the child with the full-wattage smile he rarely turned on. 'Shall I teach you an Italian game next time?'

Paolo nodded. 'Are you...Italian?'

There was a frozen, split-second pause, and Alexa had to turn her gaze away from the bitterness in Giovanni's face.

'*Si*,' he said. For now was neither the time nor the place to explain that he also had Kharastani blood running through his veins and so, by implication, did Paolo. Because that was a very big subject for a little boy to take on board. 'I am Italian—and it is the most beautiful language in the world. Did your mother never teach you any?'

'Mamma doesn't speak Italian!'

'Oh, I think you will find that she does—don't you, Lex?'

Alexa's eyes were drawn back to his face—like iron filings drawn irresistibly towards a magnet. She swallowed.

'Not any more—I've grown rusty.'

'What a pity,' he murmured, but the platitude was laced with steel. 'Every child should speak more than one language.'

Alexa ignored the silken threat underpinning his words. All she had to do was get her son safely to bed without some kind of terrible scene erupting. 'C-come on, darling,' she murmured unsteadily.

She went through Paolo's bedtime routine on autopilot. No time for a bath tonight, but tooth-brushing, hair-untangling, face-washing and story-telling took on their uniquely calming rhythm. It isn't *his* fault that stupid grown-ups had made a mess of their lives, she thought to herself fiercely as she pulled the duvet back.

But as she covered up his wiry little body—clad in soft blue pyjamas with little trains on them—she was struck by the guileless innocence in his face. Had Giovanni once looked at his mother in such a way—as if she could answer any question he put to her, solve any problem which came his way?

'I *like* that man,' confided Paolo sleepily, as he snuggled down beneath the covers and gave in to a yawn.

'Night-night, darling,' prevaricated Alexa, and wondered why her guilt should feel so intensely strong—as if someone had just flung a dank bucketload of it at her and left her dripping in it.

I did it for you, Paolo, she thought, as she gazed at where his lashes had fluttered down to form two dark arcs on his smooth, pale olive skin. *Only for you.*

Had she somehow hoped that by spinning out her goodnights Giovanni might have gone? Slipping away into the night like a bad dream?

But he had not gone anywhere. He had risen to his feet and was standing in front of the fire, with the flames behind him transforming him into a towering and threatening silhouette. She could not see the expression on his face and she didn't need to—because pure anger was radiating from him in waves almost as heated as the fire itself.

'Shut the door,' he said softly.

'Paolo—'

'I said, shut the door,' he repeated, his mouth hardening. 'Just do it.'

Alexa's hand was shaking as she complied, and she needed every bit of courage she had ever possessed as she turned round to face him.

Giovanni stared at her, observing the dark-fringed eyes and the berry-coloured mouth which trembled in dismay.

Had Alexa been hoping that by the time she came downstairs he would have gone?

His eyes bored ebony holes into her.

'So, were you ever going to tell me?' he questioned in a voice of dangerous silk.

'Giovanni—'

'Were you?' he continued. 'And—if so—when would it have been, I wonder? When he was eighteen? Maybe when he graduated? Or would it have been when he got married? Would I have been the spectre at the feast, Alexa—the unknown father turning up to curse the woman who had denied him his flesh and blood for all these years?' He lowered his voice and began to walk towards her. 'And if he had died—'

'Stop it!' she choked, clamping her hands over her ears.

'If he had died,' he continued brutally, enjoying her distress and her discomfort because, damn her—*maladizione!*—she had not cared about *his*, had she? If he could wound her with his words then he would aim for the jugular! 'What then? I would never have known, would I, Alexa? That my son had been born and had lived and died without me ever setting eyes on him?'

'No!' she moaned, because no matter how much she

tried to block the sound out his words came filtering through, hitting her like a persistent, heavy hammer.

Brutally, he wrenched her hands away from the side of her head.

'How can you live with yourself?' he continued remorselessly.

'I did it for *him*!'

'No, you lying little bitch—you did it for *you*! You did it because you wanted to keep him all to yourself!' He caught hold of her elbows, imprisoning her, and Alexa wriggled like a snake caught in a corner—wanting desperately to escape. But Giovanni was quicker than her—his reactions more alert. Without warning he levered her powerfully close up against his body, and as Alexa's eyes widened with fear and with a terrible yearning sense of recognition, he nodded his dark head.

'*Si*,' he agreed grimly. 'You feel the hardness of me? You feel how much my body wants you, even while my soul despises you for what you have done to me and to my son?' And, in a gesture born more out of anger than frustration, he drove his mouth down on hers.

For a second she struggled, but the grappling brought her even closer—so that she could feel the hard, seeking heat of his body, imprinting itself on the softness of hers. With expert pressure he prised her lips open and drove his tongue inside her mouth with a violent, stabbing movement which surely should have had her gagging, not responding—wanting greedily to kiss him back.

'Oh!' Astonished, dismayed, and so hot that she squirmed, she felt the way he arrogantly pushed up her jumper—his fingers homing in on a nipple which was almost indecently erect through the fine lace of her bra—while his other hand cupped itself over her buttock. She heard herself moan against him, felt her knees give way as a wild thought flew unbidden into her head.

Might this not absolve her from what she had done? If she gave him this, might he not find a tiny piece of his heart to forgive her? To see it her way—to try to understand the terror of losing her child to a man infinitely more powerful than a young girl on her own?

Giovanni felt his hard heat threatening to explode, and the temptation to tear down her jeans and impale her right there and then, against the wall, was overpowering. He could kiss her fraught cries quiet—feel his own power and domination as he brought her to orgasm. And as she shuddered around him he could draw comfort from his own swift conclusion—for surely the temporary obliteration of sexual pleasure was the only thing which would banish the black thoughts threatening to drive him insane?

But something stopped him. And it was not the thought that his son might hear. His *son*. Giovanni's hands dropped from her as if they had been contaminated.

'*Donnaccia*!' he hissed. Clenching his fingernails into the ball of his clenched fist, he winced, just stopping himself from drawing blood—and only then did his dark torrent of accusation flow over her. 'Slut! How many men have you allowed to take you against the wall like this, while my son slept upstairs unaware?'

CHAPTER FIVE

IT WASN'T Giovanni's abuse which brought Alexa to her senses—after all, him calling her a slut was nothing out of the ordinary, and if she didn't want him to think of her that way then she shouldn't have gone to pieces in his arms like that, should she? No, it was those two small words of utter possession which had sent hackles of fear prickling down her spine, as if someone was jabbing her with a million tiny needles.

My son, he had said. And the powerful words had been underpinned with both threat and determination.

Alexa's world was threatening to implode, and if she didn't do something soon—if she didn't take back some kind of control— then it might very well happen, and it would be too late for her to do anything about it.

'*Get away from me*,' she choked, gasping in a shuddering breath of air.

'You have a sudden change of heart? Isn't it a little late for that?' he drawled witheringly. 'Why, I could be inside you now if I had not stopped!'

His contempt was so overwhelming that Alexa felt

faint—until she forced herself to think straight. You did nothing that he didn't do, and *you are not a victim*, she told herself fiercely. And the sooner you stop acting like one, the better for all concerned—Paolo most of all.

'Can't you see why I didn't want to tell you, Giovanni?'

'No, I cannot,' he snarled. 'Never in a million years!'

'All through our marriage you accused me of sleeping with loads of men,' she said shakily.

'On the evidence of what just nearly happened, can you blame me?' he said, his mouth curving with disdain. 'Or am I to flatter myself that you've been waiting for me to walk back into your life to turn you on again?'

She tried to imagine his disbelieving scorn if she said *yes*—but that was a pointless path she had no intention of trying to set off on. Yet she had to try to make him see it from her point of view—she *had* to. Alexa steadied her breathing. 'Do you remember the last thing you said to me as I left Naples?'

'*Ciao?*' he bit out furiously.

'You said: At least we must give thanks that you aren't pregnant—for how would we ever know the identity of the father?'

There was silence for a moment while he stared at her incredulously. 'Are you telling me that you used a statement I flung at you in anger as a reason for *not telling me* that I had a son?'

'It was one of my reasons, yes.'

'And the others?' he demanded. 'Perhaps you'd like to enlighten me about what you felt gave you the right to play God with other people's lives?'

'Like your black jealousy, you mean?' she returned. 'The ridiculous accusations you kept throwing at me?' she continued steadily. 'The fact that you had me on a par with a hooker—'

'You should have *told* me you weren't a virgin!'

'I didn't realise that an unbroken hymen was a condition of marriage—or have I just been living in a different century?'

'It was your *deceit* which initiated my reaction,' he cut in icily. 'And today you have proved beyond any reasonable doubt that I was right not to trust you.'

Shaking her head with frustration, Alexa could see the great communication chasm which lay between them. They had fallen straight back into the pattern of charge and counter-charge, and nothing was going to be resolved—not in an emotionally charged situation such as this.

'I think we'd both better calm down a bit, don't you?' she questioned shakily.

At that moment Giovanni could have taken her by the shoulders and shaken her, demanding how she dared speak to him in such a way—like a teacher in charge of a naughty pupil.

Abruptly he turned on his heel and walked over to the window, which looked out onto the star-spattered night, and tried to will away the lump which had welled up in his throat and was threatening to suffocate him.

His son.

His *son*.

He stared at the tiny garden, his slow gaze taking in

a small plastic tractor which looked unreal in the silver-soaked light of the moon—and that cheap little toy seemed to symbolise all that he had lost. Or rather, all that she had stolen from him.

How long he stood there he did not know—but only when he considered he could face her without wanting to utter a torrent of invective did Giovanni turn around.

She was watching his face carefully, the enormity of her actions slowly beginning to dawn on her. She wanted to cry—but wouldn't her tears look like a self-pitying gesture from the woman whom Giovanni had always judged detrimentally and continued to judge still?

'I'm sorry—' she began, but he stanched her flow with the flat of his hand, slicing dramatically through the air—as if he was decapitating her words as she spoke them. And suddenly the path she had chosen seemed a blurred one, and she felt a great shuddering of regret. 'Maybe I should have told you about Paolo.' Her eyes searched his face in silent appeal. 'I didn't want it to turn out this way, Giovanni—honestly I didn't.'

'Oh, spare me your lies,' he grated. 'You didn't tell me, and you probably never would have done. It was only chance which brought me here today!'

'But I wrote to you once—when I was…pregnant.' She saw him flinch at her use of the word. 'Do you remember?'

His eyes narrowed. Memories were always dis-torted—*had* she written? Or was it now convenient for her to imagine she had? But, no, he *did* recall a letter—a stilted little thing, received when he was still angry and hurting and cursing his own stupidity and lack of judgement. In it she had wondered whether they might be able to have a meeting, and he had sworn, crumpled the cheap paper into a ball and hurled it into the bin.

'That bald little *note*?' he questioned. 'There was no mention of pregnancy in that, was there?'

She had been testing the waters, wanting to see if they were grown-up enough to be civil to one another. And she had been aching, too—broken by the shattering of her dreams, her heart missing the man she loved. His silence had seemed so final—and to her mixed-up way of thinking it had seemed to be for the best. He had wanted her out of his life, so why complicate matters further?

'No,' she admitted quietly. 'But you didn't reply.'

'And so for that one omission I was to be punished by being kept in ignorance of my son?'

'Giovanni—'

'No! You have no defence against my accusation because there is no defence,' he said viciously. He could see the shimmer of tears in her pale green eyes, but he hardened his heart against them. 'Why did you do it, Alexa? Do you really hate me so much?'

Hate him? She could have wept at how wrong he was. She had loved him with a passion she had never felt before, nor since.

'Not as much as you seem to hate me.'

But he seemed distracted, his eyes narrowed, as if he

were trying to keep up with his racing thoughts. 'The
past is past and we can't bring it back,' he clipped out.
'The question is—what are we going to do about it?'

She could see the calculating look in his eyes as he
though went a list of options, and Alexa felt her blood
grow cold in her veins. '*Do* about it?'

He heard her fear, and suddenly Giovanni was filled
with a sense of his own power. Did she think that she
was in complete control—the one who could make the
big decisions and have everything her own way? Up
until now, maybe—but she was about to wake up to a
lesson in reality.

'Do you really image that I am about to just walk
away?' he demanded softly.

She tried to stay calm, even though the tone of his
voice and the implacable look of determination on his
face were making her begin to panic. 'No, of course
not. But…but…'

'But what?' he queried.

'Well, it isn't going to be easy, is it? If you want to
see Paolo.'

'*If* I want to see Paolo?' he echoed dangerously.

'Well, yes—I mean, you live in Italy and I live in
England. We're going to have to consult lawyers about
access, aren't we? Draw up some kind of agreement.'

A nerve flickered in Giovanni's cheek. Did she
realise that with her dust-dry statement about lawyers
she had concentrated his mind perfectly? he wondered.
That her tentative but lukewarm attempt at appease-
ment had helped seal her fate?

His black eyes glittered. 'You have had things your way for far too long, *cara*, and that is all about to change.'

'What do you mean?' She could hear the fear in her voice, and she saw from the glint of triumph in his eyes that he heard it too.

'I want to take my son to Kharastan to meet his grandfather,' he stated flatly.

Alexa stared at him. Her first thought was that she had played this all wrong—and please couldn't she have the time-tape back to rewind it? But how far back would she go? To before this afternoon? Or before she had her baby? Maybe she would take it back even further than that—so that she would never have gone to Italy and never met him in the first place.

She could hear the pounding of her heart, and feel the corresponding dryness of her mouth. 'Giovanni, please let's not be hasty.'

'Hasty? You have some kind of nerve! You've had nearly five years, and now you're trying to waste yet more time?' He took a deep breath, enjoying the sudden panic which had clouded her eyes. 'Well, I'm sorry— that isn't an option. I've missed enough, and I don't intend to miss a second more. I'm taking Paolo with me.'

Giovanni realised that the subject which had dominated his thoughts until a couple of hours ago had now begun to develop different repercussions.

He was son and heir to a sheikh. But this was no longer just an isolated piece of information, to do with as he wished. The momentous discovery of his own birthright would impact on his son, he realised.

His *son*!

'You can't just pluck a child from the English countryside and transplant him to some exotic place he's never even heard of!' she protested.

'I want to take him to Kharastan,' he repeated stubbornly. 'And I'm going to.'

Alexa could see from the obdurate look on his face that he meant it, and she realised that she was going to have to be very careful. 'He won't come without me,' she pointed out softly.

His answering look could have withered at ten paces, but she forced herself not to recoil beneath its onslaught.

'Then you shall come too,' he said silkily. As he had originally intended—and, sweet heaven, she would pay for what she had done.

'And if I refuse?'

'You can't refuse.' His mouth curved. 'You have no choice, Alexa. Unless you want an all-out war, with our son as the spoils, then I advise you to co-operate with me.'

'With our son as the *spoils*?' she echoed. 'Like some kind of *trophy*? If that's how you see him—'

'That is enough!' His voice cut through her protest like a guillotine. 'You have been playing God all his life— you can hardly blame me if I've now decided to do the same.' He raked his fingers through his thick dark hair, his hard-edged smile laced with triumph. 'The wedding is early next week. We shall fly out there together.'

She felt dizzy and frightened at his use of the word *we*—because it almost made them sound as if they were a real family, and nothing could be further from the truth. How words could paint such false and haunting images inside your head, she thought, as a great wave of sadness overwhelmed her. 'What about my job? And what am I going to tell Paolo?'

With uncharacteristic hesitation Giovanni mulled over the possibilities—but he had not added to his monumental success without knowing that sometimes you had to step back. At the moment he was nothing other than a curiosity to the boy, and he had no influence on him. At least, not yet—though all that would soon change. Again he felt the clench of something like pain around his heart, and his eyes gleamed dark accusation at her.

'That is your problem, *cara*, not mine.'

CHAPTER SIX

'WAKE up, darling. Wake up.'

Jet-black curls moved beneath Alexa's stroking hand, and Paolo stirred as the sound of the jet's engines changed, indicating that they were beginning their descent into Kharastan.

'He'll come to in a minute,' she said, aware that Giovanni was watching her every movement, those keen black eyes weighing up everything she did, as they had done for the whole seven-hour flight, and before that as well. She felt as if she was undergoing some silent and tough assessment—as if he was examining her behaviour as a mother to see if she came up to his exacting standards. No, Giovanni hasn't changed, Alexa thought despairingly—but you aren't going to let him get to you.

He had picked them up first thing that morning, in a shiny black chauffeur-driven car which had had all the neighbours gawping before it whisked them off to a nearby airstrip, where one of Sheikh Zahir's private jets had been waiting for them.

It was the first time Paolo had ever been on an aeroplane—and Alexa sincerely hoped that he wasn't going to measure every future flight against this one. She was no experienced traveller herself, but this aircraft of the Sheikh's fleet was something outside the experience of most people—herself included. The exterior of the plane was dazzling white and sleek as a bird, while its interior was all restrained luxury, with gleaming woods and pure gold fittings.

There were low divans on which you could sleep, a dining area complete with table and overhead chandelier, a seating section where pure silk embroidered cushions were heaped upon squishy sofas, and a bathroom which wouldn't have looked out of place in a luxury hotel.

It seemed that everything they desired could be catered for—from soft-boiled eggs to lamb chops—but Alexa had asked if they could try some typical Kharastani cuisine, thinking that it might be a good idea to get Paolo used to the local food, while he was slightly over-awed with the lavishness of the plane.

She had seen Giovanni's eyes narrow as they'd met hers, and he had given a reluctant nod of his dark head in response. Alexa hadn't been looking for his approval, but she wouldn't have been human if she hadn't enjoyed it when it came.

Yes, Paolo had loved every second of the flight—which was more than could be said for her. Because for her the most part had been like tiptoeing through a minefield of unasked questions and forbidden subjects—made worse when their son had decided to nestle in his seat and sleep.

At least while he was awake there was some degree of civility between her and Giovanni—rather than the thinly disguised friction which was bubbling away beneath the surface like a cauldron of unwanted and unexpressed emotions. It was almost as if neither of them dared approach the more difficult topics—as if to do so might start some mid-air row which would embarrass them and frighten Paolo, or give the discreet crew something to frown upon.

The sudden drone of the engines told Giovanni that soon they would be stepping into a strange and beautiful land—peopled by an exotic nation of strong, black-eyed men he might have ruled had Fate not decreed it differently.

'What have you told him, Lex?' asked Giovanni softly, as he watched the boy begin to stir from sleep and he felt the increasingly familiar pang of disbelief and delight that this long-limbed child should have sprung from his loins.

She heard the urgency and the faintly proprietorial note in his voice, and once more it gave Alexa cause for concern. How far would he go to get what he wanted? she wondered. And how much of Paolo *did* he want? What if he decided that a four-year-old boy was a pain, and he most definitely *didn't* want to be a hands-on parent?

Yet deep in her heart Alexa knew this was a no-hoper—she had only to see the rapt look on her estranged husband's face to understand that. It was as if he couldn't get enough of staring at his son—displaying that sense of a newly formed love-affair which almost every parent had for their child.

'So, what have you told Paolo about me?' he repeated.

'I haven't mentioned you specifically.' She saw the look of simmering fury which hardened his dark face. 'He knows we're going to Kharastan—I told him we're going to a very special wedding in a royal palace. With you.'

'And what did he say?'

'He asked when we were going.'

'He didn't ask *why*?' he questioned incredulously.

Alexa shook her head. 'Children think differently to adults.'

It was the wrong thing to say.

'I wouldn't know, would I?' he declared hotly. He saw the colour flare in her cheeks and he knew that his barb had thrust home. 'So, how exactly are you *going* to explain to him? He needs to know who I am, Alexa—and we need to agree some kind of strategy for telling him.'

She felt her blood run cold. How quickly things could change. Twenty-four hours and he considered it his right to be included in decision-making. *We*, he had said—and just the sound of it had sent shivers running down her spine. But how could she prevent it?

'Not yet,' she said.

'You're hedging.'

'I'm thinking about Paolo.'

'No,' he contradicted forcefully. 'You are not. If you were thinking of Paolo then you might have stopped to consider his needs—and all children need a father!'

'Even if that father has judged a woman and found her wanting in a way that they used to do in Medieval times?' she declared. 'Who puts a woman on a pedestal so high that there is no way for her to go other than crashing down?'

'But you played the innocent to ensnare me, didn't you?' he accused softly. 'And I was fool enough to fall for it—mesmerised by the bewitching fall of red-gold hair and those green eyes which sparkled so innocently.'

'I did not *lure* you,' she said proudly. 'I never *said* I was a virgin.'

'Yet you knew how important it was to me.' Was it the fact he had grown up to the sound of men creeping in late at night as his mother brought her latest young lover home which made him place a higher price than most Italian men on the question of purity? 'You tricked me!'

'No.' Alexa bit her lip. 'I was too young and inexperienced to ever *dream* of concocting such a fabrication.' Too much in love and in awe of this masterly man.

'So why didn't you tell me, Lex?'

'Because our relationship was about *romance*—or at least I thought it was. Not a clinical breakdown of past partners—and don't forget I'd had only one!'

A nerve flickered in his cheek. His time with Alexa had been the only time in his life he had allowed himself to believe in the supposed fairytale of love. 'Not romance,' he snapped. 'I'd call it fantasy. You *pretended*, Lex—you know you did!'

'You never asked! It seemed somehow…*tacky* to discuss something so clinical. You made me feel like the only woman who mattered. I thought you wanted to prolong the anticipation—the glorious agony of making us wait,' she whispered. 'I didn't realise that you would have such double standards—that it was okay for you to have had loads of lovers, but my one solitary sexual encounter would be the launching pad for a whole heap of unreasonable accusations. I was either virgin or whore in your eyes, Giovanni—a stereotype, not a real woman.'

'A *real* woman would not have kept my son hidden away from me,' he said stonily.

Alexa drew a deep breath. 'I did what seemed best at the time. I was wrong. I'm sorry.'

He flashed her a cold black look. 'You've decided that now is a good time to apologise?' he mocked. 'Buying yourself brownie points while you can, are you, Lex?'

Oh, what was the use? Alexa sat back in her seat, closing her eyes tiredly as she thought of the sleepless nights she'd spent since he had walked back into her life.

For nights now she had lain awake and seriously pondered the possibility of just gathering up a few vital belongings and fleeing from Lymingham with Paolo— away from Giovanni and all the complications his return had thrown up. It hadn't been a lack of adventure which had stopped her, but the certain knowledge that she could have run to the ends of the earth and he would find her, now that he had discovered his son. And something else had stopped her, too—something that she had not expected to strike her so forcefully.

The fact that she could no longer deny Paolo what was rightfully his—a father.

But how did you *tell* a child something like that? How did you explain in words a four-year-old could understand just why she had never mentioned him

before—and in such a way that she would not paint a
black picture of Giovanni? Because that wouldn't be fair
to either of them. And wasn't another reason behind her
reluctance to tell Paolo the slight fear that her son would
lash out and be angry with her? Was Giovanni right,
after all—was she letting her own self-interest govern
her behaviour to the detriment of her son?

'You're going to have to say something to him soon!'
Giovanni's voice broke into her troubled thoughts.
'Because other people already know.'

Alexa opened her eyes. 'What do you mean?
Which people?'

'I have told Malik—the Sheikh's aide. Some explanation was necessary,' he said grimly. 'How else could
I explain why I suddenly wanted to bring a child with
me? And Sheikh Zahir will also have been told by now.
And word will get out, particularly when we arrive.' His
black eyes sparkled with a hurt he hid behind the patina
of a readily accessible anger. 'Even if I had said nothing
onlookers would have to be pretty unobservant not to
make the connection—given the likeness between us.'

'No, I guess not,' she said slowly, her mind full of
conflicting thoughts. Because—if she was truthful—
wasn't that another thing which freaked her out?
Similarity was perhaps the wrong description—mirror-
image might be more accurate, because Paolo was a
lminiature version of his father.

Alexa glanced down at the dozing child. True,
Paolo's skin had not quite the same dark lustre of his
father's—but the jet hair with the hint of a curl to it, and

the elegant and patrician features were the same. And the eyes… It was the deep dark eyes which matched most precisely—slanting and intelligent and framed with a thick sweep of black lashes which most women would have paid a fortune to possess.

With her contrasting pale and golden looks Alexa could not detect a single physical characteristic that she shared with her son, and it left her feeling something of an outsider. Like the unsuspecting bird who had nurtured a cuckoo's chick in her nest. *And now she was afraid that Paolo was going to fly away—to a glamorous new life of palaces and sheikhs—while his shop assistant mother faded ever more distantly into the background.*

'So, what are you going to say to him?' he demanded.

Alexa cast a fleeting look at Paolo, who had fallen back into a deep sleep in the way children seemed able to do in the blink of an eye. She was sure he couldn't hear—but didn't they say that hearing was the most acute of all the senses?

She placed her finger over her lips, but Giovanni shook his head.

Did she think she could shush him because of the child's proximity, and thus avoid discussing topics which needed addressing? Nice try. His mouth curved into a hard smile.

'If you don't want to be overheard, then come and speak to me in private.' He rose to his feet and walked over to the far end of the luxury cabin, well out of earshot of his son—and arrogantly beckoned to her.

For a moment she thought of defying him. But almost in the same moment realised that it would be a complete waste of time. Because Giovanni held all the cards, she realised. They were on one of the Sheikh's flight and he was the son of the Sheikh: the honoured guest. Whereas she was merely a means to an end.

She had something he wanted—his initial desire for a sexual partner had been superseded by something far more important. Now he wanted their little boy. With a sinking heart, Alexa realised she was effectively trapped—and it had nothing to do with being in the enclosed space of an aircraft. She was going to be as trapped when they landed in Kharastan as she had felt during her short, ill-fated marriage.

But in the meantime she had her son's feelings and welfare to consider, and the question Giovanni had asked was important. How *was* she going to tell him? If Alexa could have buried her head in the sand and prayed for the whole issue to just disappear, then she would have done. But it wasn't going to, because Giovanni wouldn't let it—and even Alexa recognised that it would be wrong to do so.

She recognised too that the most damaging way it could emerge would be if it was blurted out during a row just before they landed. So there was little choice other than to unclip her seat-belt and walk reluctantly over to join the man she had married, trying without success to ignore the fact that her heart still clenched with longing whenever she looked at him.

Today he was dressed entirely in black, in an exqui-

sitely cut suit which hugged his lean body and emphasised the long, muscular shaft of his legs. His shirt was
dark too, and he wore no tie. He looked expensive and
dangerous, with the faintest suggestion of shadow at his
jaw—a potent symbol of his virility.

As she grew closer to him she could smell the faint
yet distinctive tang of the aftershave he had always used,
and even as it prompted some terrible yearning deep
inside her Alexa despaired that she could even be
thinking of something like that at such an emotionally
fraught time.

'So, what are you going to say and when are you
going to say it?' he demanded softly. 'I suggest soon—
the sooner the better.'

'With…' Alexa swallowed. 'With you present, you
mean?'

He stared at her from narrowed eyes, and at that
moment Giovanni's anger became a rage which threatened to explode like champagne from a bottle which had
been shaken furiously.

'What did you imagine?' he breathed. 'That I would
conveniently allow you to give him your version of 'the
truth' in secret? To paint me as some dark monster from
your past?'

'I wouldn't dream of doing something like that!' she
defended on a whisper.

'No? Just what *have* you told him about the fact that
he doesn't have a father?'

In a way she had been expecting this question, in all
its painful complexity. 'I just told him the truth. That his

Mummy got married, but sadly the marriage didn't work out.' Alexa shrugged her shoulders in a brittle movement, because the matter-of-fact statement did nothing to convey her deep sadness and the sense of failure she felt that their marriage had disintegrated.

'What a perfect explanation,' he put in sarcastically. 'Did he never ask questions?'

Alexa shook her head. 'He seemed to accept that. Lots of his friends have parents who are divorced—'

'Ah, yes, of course! What a conveniently disposable world we live in,' he interrupted, in a low, savage voice. 'Maybe the reason he didn't ask any more was because he could see you didn't want to talk about it. Children are very good at picking up on the mood of adults and acting accordingly.'

Alexa opened her mouth to stand up for what she had done but thought better of it—and it had nothing to do with fearing Giovanni's wrath, but a with sudden insight as to where some of his anger might be coming from. Because for the first time she realised that she had denied Paolo a father in the same way that Giovanni's own father had been denied him, and the enormity of that now hit her.

She whispered her words. 'I acted the only way I could at the time—'

'And I've told you before,' he cut in viciously, 'that I neither want nor need your expedient explanations. Don't start coming over all penitent now, Alexa—just to make life easier for yourself!'

'What would *you* have said?' she questioned painfully.

Verbally, he wanted to rail and lash out at her with the might of his tongue. But the sleeping child on the other side of the luxurious cabin inhibited him.

'Alas, men are rarely in the privileged position that women occupy in a child's life. They cannot spirit their offspring away and airbrush the other parent from history!'

She wanted to explain. To tell him that she had been frightened—genuinely frightened—of his rages and his power and possessiveness. But if she admitted that fear now then wouldn't it acknowledge a weakness which still existed today? And surely Giovanni would simply capitalise on that weakness, using it as a springboard to exact some kind of revenge for what she had done?

'I'll tell him when the moment is right,' she promised.

'You will tell him when he wakes up.'

'Is that an order?'

'What do you think, *cara mia*? That I would beg and plead or wait at *your* convenience?'

Their gazes locked. Ebony fire sizzled from his and seemed to burn into her soul itself. But Alexa knew that she had to be strong or Giovanni would try to take everything. A long time ago he had already stolen her heart—but she would not let him have her son, or her sanity.

'Mamma!'

Alexa smiled. 'What is it, darling? Did you sleep well?'

'Are we nearly there yet?' asked Paolo, blinking his eyes open and looking around him.

'Nearly,' said Alexa. 'Why don't you come over here and have a look out of the window?'

Paolo jumped up and came to stand next to her. 'Look, Mamma!' He pointed his finger excitedly. '*Look!*'

'They're mountains,' said Alexa, looking down and realising they were flying over the a place she had thought existed only within the prohibitively expensive sections of travel magazines. 'Huge, snow-capped mountains.'

'And, look—there is the desert,' said a soft, deep voice.

Alexa swallowed, for Giovanni had come to stand behind them, and she could feel his presence—could almost touch it and taste it. The scent of him—his own unique, musky scent—pervaded her nostrils and replaced the air with the essence of *him*.

Didn't they say that women were attracted to alpha-men by some subtle processing mechanism which happened on a subliminal level? Was that what had happened—her body had taken into account all the factors which would ensure that she picked the strongest, most virile of the bunch? She wanted to shout at him—*please stay away from me!* Yet she wanted him to gather her in his arms too. To pull her close to his hard, seeking heat and cover her mouth with his kisses. Rough kisses that would not give her clamouring conscience time to resist.

'Can you see it, Paolo?' he murmured, leaning closer in, for he could tell from her posture that she was acutely aware of him. Was she uncomfortable with him standing so close to her? Did she want him? Good!

Their son's attention was completely taken up with the flash of silver and white buildings, and deliberately

Giovanni pushed his body into hers. Could she feel the hard ridge of his erection pushing against her bottom? He heard her barely perceptible intake of breath, felt the briefest shudder of her slim body, and knew an answering moment of heady triumph which more than made up for the ache of frustration. Yes, she wanted him!

Moving away from her, he heard the faint hiss as she expelled the breath she had been holding, and he bent his head close to his son's. 'Do you know why we're going to Kharastan, Paolo?' he asked gently.

' 'Cos there's a wedding!'

'Do you know whose wedding it is?'

Paolo shook his dark curls, and more of them fell around his head in disarray. 'No.'

'It is Xavier's wedding.'

'Who is Xa-Xa-Xavier?' stumbled Paolo.

'He is my brother.' Giovanni reached down and tangled his fingers in the silken mop of curls, and to Alexa's astonishment Paolo let him. 'Well, he is my half-brother—we have the same father, but different mothers.'

'Two girls in my class have that!'

Giovanni nodded. 'Lots of people have that these days—but I only found out that I had a brother very, very recently.'

Paolo's eyes widened as he stared up at Giovanni. '*Did* you?'

'*Si*,' said Giovanni softly, and then crouched down so that his eyes were on a level with the boy's. He felt his heart lurch. 'Sometimes families get all complicated for all kinds of reasons.'

He smiled at the little boy then, and Alexa was taken aback by the affectionate brilliance of that smile. It hurt when she compared it to the way he looked at her. But this isn't about me, she reminded herself. This is about Paolo, and the best way to tell him, and if you don't act now then Giovanni is just going to go right ahead and tell him.

'Paolo, what Giovanni is trying to tell you is that—'

'I am your father.'

The words rang out, and seeming to echo around the enclosed space, and Alexa bit her lip so hard that she felt the salt taste of blood. So he had done it anyway.

There was silence, and Giovanni was appalled that he should feel suffused with such *triumph* when he saw the hurt and the pain which clouded her green eyes. But she hurt me too, he thought viciously. She has hurt me more than I ever thought possible. She doesn't have the monopoly on inflicting pain.

Swiftly, he cast these reflections aside and stared into Paolo's little face, hoping—no, actually *praying*—that coming straight out with the truth had been the best way to handle it.

Alexa stood waiting too, feeling like an outsider—a shadowy interloper who was intruding on a very private conversation.

'Paolo?' she questioned tentatively.

Her son looked up at her then, and on his face was an expression she had never seen before. It was a mixture of emotions—of curiosity and relief and very definitely *delight*—but it was a troubled and faintly reproachful face, too.

'But Mamma doesn't have a husband,' he protested.

'Yes, I do,' she said, in a low voice she prayed would not tremble and crack. 'Giovanni is my husband. We got married—'

'In a fever?' Giovanni cut in cruelly.

'A long time ago,' Alexa followed on evenly. 'And we kind of…well, we lost touch.' She waited for Giovanni to contradict her, but to her surprise he did no such thing. The glint in his black eyes told her he had not forgiven her—but he had no intention of letting their son suffer because *their* relationship was in a mess.

Paolo seemed blissfully unaware of the undercurrents of tension sizzling in the air all around them, and the huge implications behind why she had *not* told him. His eyes were the size of chocolate saucers as he stared up in wonder at the tall, elegant man with the dark, rugged face. 'You're my *daddy*?'

There was a lump, and it was a pretty big one, which had just lodged itself right in the middle of his throat, so all Giovanni could do was nod, his lips pressing hard against one another as he attempted to keep his feelings in check.

'Yes, I am,' he said eventually. 'I'm your Papà.'

Alexa stood frozen, looking at the unfamiliar sight of his arrogant and beautiful face struggling beneath the weight of unfamiliar emotions. Like a spectator at some shamelessly weepy movie, she watched as he held his arms open and Paolo went straight into them—like someone coming home after a long absence—and she wondered just where they went from here.

From the things he'd said—and the contempt which had snapped from his voice—she guessed that Giovanni would never find it in his heart to forgive her.

The question was, would Paolo?

CHAPTER SEVEN

THE hot Kharastani sun beat down on Alexa's head, and she blinked as the young woman wearing a filmy veil over her moon-pale hair joined the tips of her fingers together as if in prayer and bowed deeply from the waist

'May I have the honour of welcoming you to the Blue Palace, Alexa?' she said, in a soft, low voice. 'My name is Sorrel, and I shall be looking after you while you are here.'

Just when Alexa had reassured herself that there couldn't possibly be any *more* surprises lying in wait, she had been proved wrong yet again—because here was another. And maybe it was good to have something to focus on other than all the possible repercussions of Paolo finding out that Giovanni was his father. 'But you're English!' she exclaimed, looking at the blonde in surprise.

Sorrel—who looked about the same age as Alexa— gave a wide smile. 'You can tell? I don't have any trace of a Kharastani accent?'

Alexa shook her head. 'Not to my ears,' she said, and

then looked around her with a slightly uncertain air, as if she expected to wake up from this crazy dream at any minute and find herself back in her little rented cottage in Lymingham. But, no, she was here—with an imposingly domed and turreted building behind her, the largest of all the royal residences in Kharastan.

On arrival at the palace Paolo had immediately wanted the bathroom. He had insisted that Giovanni take him—not her—and Alexa had fought an inner battle before giving in gracefully.

'It is easier that way,' said Sorrel softly, as they watched a silken-robe-clad servant lead Giovanni and his son through some carved doors. 'For there are areas of the palace which are still off-limits to women.'

Alexa nodded, telling herself that her son's behaviour was understandable in the circumstances—even if it was with a conviction she didn't really feel.

Paolo had just discovered a father figure and he wanted to make the most of it. Like a child who had been given a wonderful new toy—he simply wanted to play with it non-stop. And, if you considered that they had just arrived in an exotic, very different country from the one he was used to—a country which seemed to be dominated by the male of the species—then surely she could understand why her son wanted to look and act like one of the men?

So why did she feel so alone and so excluded? As if she was standing on the very edge of a cliff which was slowly crumbling beneath her feet? Because the balance of power had changed, she recognised painfully. It was all now heavily weighted in Giovanni's favour—and, oh, hadn't he just taken to his new royal status as to the manner born?

A fleet of cars had met them at the airport when they had touched down in the capital—long, low cars, with tinted windows and bullet-proofed bodywork—and from these had emerged men with bulky jackets and dark, impenetrable eyes whose gaze never quite met hers.

They had been welcomed by an official who wore flowing ivory robes. His name was Fariq and he was secretary to Malik—the Sheikh's most senior and trusted aide. He had bowed to Giovanni.

'The Akil Malik bids me tell you that he is currently in discussion with Sheikh Khalim of Maraban, prior to the royal wedding. He sends his most abject apologies and will see you later, at dinner.'

As they climbed into one of the luxury cars, Alexa turned to Giovanni with a frown.

'Everyone's treating you as a member of the royal family,' she said in confusion.

Giovanni shrugged, determined to remain friendly towards her—at least outwardly, and especially when they were with Paolo. The boy would not know a moment of disharmony if Giovanni could prevent it—and neither would he be told how close he had come to never knowing the identity of his father. It had been Alexa's doing, but no blame would be apportioned there. What was the point, when the child adored his mother? To demonise her would only make Giovanni the monster in Paolo's young eyes.

No, he would make Alexa pay for her deception in

his own particular way—and he knew exactly how he was going to do it. Anticipation heated his blood. He could feel it flaring warm over his cheekbones. But the glance he threw her was nothing but mocking as he enjoyed her obvious discomfiture, the fact that she could not seem to relax beside him.

'That is because they have *accepted* me as a member of the royal family,' he said coolly.

'So soon?' she asked.

'It was decided that waiting would serve no good purpose,' he drawled, as Paolo climbed on to his knee and snuggled into him like an eager puppy. 'Thus my identity as the second son of the Sheikh has been revealed in the last few days.'

But Giovanni's cool air disguised his own utter astonishment at the news which had reached him via reports sent directly by Malik. The Kharastani people—who adored their ruling family and anyone connected to it—had taken to Giovanni immediately.

No matter that the circumstances of his birth had been unusual, to say the least—it made no difference to the enthusiasm of the country's reaction.

The *Kharastan Observer* had produced a thoughtful editorial, celebrating the new blood being brought to the line by Xavier and now Giovanni.

Any son of Zahir with Kharastani blood running through his veins is sheikh enough for the people of this land. And if two heirs have been produced, then our people will know the meaning of a true bargain!

It had been planned that Giovanni should make his first official appearance on the balcony, following the royal wedding. His mouth hardened into a determined line. And he fully intended to hold Paolo aloft in his arms!

Alexa grew silent during the car journey to the palace—feeling as if she was at the beginning of a process intended to edge her towards obscurity. Paolo was wriggling on Giovanni's knee, chattering excitedly as they passed strange flowering trees through which they could see skies much bigger than the skies back home.

'Look at the soldiers!' cried Paolo. 'They've got *guns*!'

Alexa shot Giovanni a beseeching look.

His eyes narrowed, but he touched Paolo's arm lightly. 'See over here instead,' he murmured. 'There is a little monkey—playing on an accordion.'

'Oooh!'

'And do you know that there are snake-charmers in the main square of the city?'

'*Real* snakes?'

Giovanni nodded. 'Black cobras—and pythons.'

'Can I see them?'

'I'm sure you can, and, look—here we are. Just coming up to the palace.'

'A palace?' questioned Paolo, who had only ever seen them pictured in his story books.

'A palace,' agreed Giovanni solemnly. 'It is where the Sheikh lives, and soon you shall meet him for yourself.' Across the top of Paolo's head, his eyes once more met Alexa's. The child wouldn't have made the association, but had she? Sheikh Zahir was his grandfather. Paolo too had royal blood running in his veins. And to the people of Kharastan this connection would be valued more highly than the purest gold.

'Is *that* it?' Paolo piped up excitedly.

'It certainly is.' He smiled.

Giovanni had stayed at the Blue Palace during his last visit, but this time he was stunned into a kind of dazed silence—as if the true magnificence of the building was only evident on a second careful viewing, and by imagining it through a child's eyes. He realised with something of a start that he was not used to looking at something from another person's perspective.

'Oh, it's beautiful,' breathed Alexa as she looked out of the limousine window, all her troubles momentarily dissolved by the impact the building made on her senses. 'Utterly beautiful.'

Every shade of blue she had ever seen—and a few more besides—was there, culminating in a soaring dome which tantalised the eyes. The combination of blues made a colour so intense that it rivalled anything produced by nature. But, in contrast, the flowers which grew everywhere were many-hued—pinks and reds and purples and creams, and the deep saffron shade of egg yolk. The powerful scent from the massed blooms pervaded her senses as they climbed out of the car, and made her feel weak.

And that was when the blonde woman called Sorrel had appeared from within the shadowed sanctuary of the palace to welcome them—looking so cool and ethereal in her gossamer-fine veil that Alexa had half wondered if she might have dreamt her up.

Alexa found herself wishing that she had worn a hat, or something a little cooler than the linen trousers and jacket she had worn—but she had been too self-conscious to wear anything more ethnic to Heathrow Airport.

'Come inside, into the cool and the shade,' Sorrel urged. 'You look hot.'

'I *am* hot,' Alexa confessed. And tired and disenchanted—and terrified that I'm going to lose my son to a man who once said he loved me but now looks at me with nothing but hatred in his black eyes. Licking her dry lips, and feeling ever more disorientated, Alexa looked at the blonde woman. 'H-how come you speak English so perfectly?' she enquired, in a voice which sounded wobbly.

A faint crease appeared between Sorrel's brows. 'I shall tell you everything you wish to know—but you are in no fit state to ask or answer questions at the moment. Come with me and I shall direct you to your suite. There you can bathe and change into something more suitable for our climate.'

'But I'm waiting for my son,' protested Alexa.

'Your son will be fine,' soothed Sorrel. 'I promise you. One of the servants will bring him to you—the best thing that you could do for him would be to have yourself some rest. You look dead on your feet.'

Could Alexa trust Sorrel? More importantly—could she trust Giovanni to look after Paolo? Alexa was feeling light-headed now, and yet she knew with a bone-deep certainty that Paolo would be safe.

'Maybe you're right,' she said shakily.

Sorrel led her along a series of seemingly endless and interlinking marble corridors. Alexa felt as if she was in a honeycomb. At the very heart of the palace was a central courtyard, which contained the most exquisite garden Alexa had ever seen.

Yellow flowers tumbled down through the branches of tall trees which provided welcome shade, and there were waxy white flowers which filled the air with their heady scent. The paths which divided the garden into a series of rooms were of blue and white mosaic tiles, and the sweet, swishing sound of a fountain playing made Alexa long to jump into the refreshing water.

'These are your rooms,' said Sorrel, throwing open a set of double doors.

Inside was a huge salon, with faded silk rugs and exquisite inlaid furniture, and chandeliers which glittered like a million diamond icicles suspended from the ceiling.

'There are two bedrooms and three bathrooms,' said Sorrel softly. 'Perhaps,' she added gently, 'you might wish to freshen up?'

There was a part of Alexa which was past protesting at the way her life seemed to have been taken over. She was so weary—emotionally *and* physically, that even putting one foot in front of the other seemed to take the most monumental effort.

'But Paolo—'

'I suspect that Xavier is on his way to meet him and Giovanni to give the child a quick tour of the palace— it will help him get orientated—so you certainly have time to change.' Her face softened. 'Better Paolo sees his mother refreshed and with a smile on her face.'

A smile? Was it possible to smile whole-heartedly when inside you felt as if your heart was breaking?

'Look,' said Sorrel softly, and guided her towards a lovely oval mirror which hung on one of the walls. 'See for yourself.'

Alexa stared back at herself, and if she hadn't already been as white as a wedding veil she might have blanched from the shock. She looked *frightful*. Apart from the dispirited set of her shoulders, her eyes were tired, and there was a dark streak of something across her cheek, where she must have run the back of her hand—now, why hadn't Giovanni told her about *that*? Because he wanted her to look a fool? The shop girl she really was—out of place in such lavish surroundings?

Was he hoping she would make such a bad impression that the Sheikh and other members of his newfound family would consider her unfit to be the mother of a child with royal blood?

If Alexa had thought Giovanni powerful enough to snatch her son away from her—she hadn't even considered what it would be like to have the full might of the Kharastani royal family banked against her.

But along with her fear came a renewed wave of determination. Was she just going to play into his hands? To sit back and let it happen?

Like hell she was!

'Why is an Englishwoman such as yourself living in this strange and exotic place, Sorrel?' she questioned quietly, because the other woman's kindness was making her warm to her.

'My father was the British ambassador here in Kharastan for many years,' said Sorrel. 'I spent all my vacations out here, and I quickly learned the language and a love for its people.' A cloud passed over her beautiful face. 'My parents were killed in an aircraft over the mountains of Maraban when I was sixteen, and I was made the ward of Malik, the Sheikh's aide—a very important man, whom you will meet later.'

'You didn't want to go back to live in England?' questioned Alexa, fascinated by a story which momentarily made her own troubles fade into the background.

Sorrel shook her head. 'Not a bit. I felt an indescribable *affinity* with Kharastan,' she said earnestly. 'Maybe I learned that from my parents, who taught me much about its culture and its turbulent history, and I was lucky enough to be fluent in the language, which is rare for a Western woman. Whenever I was in England I seemed to live for my time here—so I decided to complete my schooling and university here.' She shrugged her narrow shoulders and gave a shy smile. 'And here I am.'

'So what is your role here now?' asked Alexa tentatively.

'Ah, my role.' Sorrel gave a dry laugh. 'I work at the British Embassy and live within the palace walls. I do not think a definition exists for my role here!'

Alexa wondered about the slightly acid tone which had coloured Sorrel's voice, but told herself it was none of her business. She certainly had enough on her own plate to worry about. Yet the other woman's words had been kind and encouraging—she had not appeared to mind Alexa's interest. Was it too much to hope for a tentative sisterhood between herself and her fellow countrywoman? An alliance, perhaps?

'Are Giovanni, Paolo and I all staying in this suite together?' she asked Sorrel softly.

'Yes.' There was a barely perceptible pause. 'That was what Giovanni requested.' Sorrel's face was impassive and she gave a helpless shrug. *Don't blame me*, it seemed to say. *Don't ask me questions I cannot in conscience answer.*

And Alexa understood perfectly. Sorrel's silent gesture was telling her something she had already guessed—that Giovanni had all the power here, and his wishes would be paramount. There was little choice for Alexa other than to go along with it.

But that didn't mean that he could actually take her child from her by force.

If she was about to have a custody fight on her hands, then Giovanni had better realise that a mother's love could move mountains. Yet, just as a general going into battle would not do so if he was weary and unkempt, so neither could Alexa meet anyone while she was looking like this.

'Can I have a quick bath?' she asked Sorrel.

'A quick bath!' Sorrel laughed. 'I haven't heard someone say that since I was at boarding school in England, many years ago! Yes, of course you can—I took the liberty of having one drawn for you in preparation.'

And, despite her distracted state, Alexa couldn't help but exclaim out loud when Sorrel opened the door to one of the bathrooms and she saw the vast circular bathtub, lined with inlaid mosaic. The water within it was sweetly scented, and there were rose petals floating on the steaming surface.

'Like something out of the *Arabian Nights*?' guessed Sorrel, with a smile. 'It's not exactly asses' milk, but I think you'll enjoy it.'

Enjoy it?

After Sorrel had left, Alexia pulled off her crumpled clothes and slipped into the perfumed waters, letting out a long, instinctive sigh of pleasure. The bath was almost deep enough to float in, and never had the sensation of warm water embracing her wearing limbs seemed so utterly pleasurable. She could have stayed there all day. But she didn't have all day—so she washed her hair and then pulled on a fluffy towelling robe and tried not to compare this to her small bathroom at home, where she had to contort yourself like an ostrich to dry herself off, and where Paolo's socks and pants hung on a drying stand during the winter months.

Her case had been produced and unpacked in the dressing room, and hanging in the wardrobe were Alexa's brand-new clothes. Before the trip she had gone online and discovered what was acceptable garb in Kharastan—and then she'd left Paolo with the child-minder and hit the fabulous Asian bazaar which visited her corner of southern England once a month.

For a song, Alexa been able to purchase swatches of

silks in different colours, which she had made up into close approximations of the long, floaty tunics Kharastani women wore. Now she picked out one of them and ran her fingertips over a light material, the most delicate and gossamer-fine silk, and couldn't wait to slip it on.

Pulling on the delicate fabric, she heard it whisper in a silken kiss over her warm skin, and just at that moment she felt almost decadent—not like the responsible and nun-like single mother she had become out of necessity. *This isn't real*, she told herself in slight desperation. *None of this is real.*

With one final glance in the mirror, she walked back through into the dim light of the suite and went to find her son.

Narrowing her eyes against the bright light which blazed outside, she looked around to see Paolo sitting at a table on the wide terrace, drinking through a straw from a glass of juice the colour of a sunset, watched by a young Kharastani woman who was clearly some kind of nanny figure.

At the sound of Alexa's footsteps he turned his dark head, his eyes lighting up as he scrambled down from the chair, running full-pelt into her arms and squealing with excitement.

'Mamma, Mamma! The garden is much bigger than the park at home!'

'Is it? Oh, Paolo.' She tightened her arms around him and closed her eyes. 'How are you, my darling?'

He wriggled free from the constriction of her

motherly embrace. 'I saw the palace an' it's *huge*, and I met Uncle X-Xavier, an' there's a toy box in my bedroom, an' we can have sore-bet for dinner!'

'What's sore-bet?'

'He means sorbet,' came a low, silky voice from behind them, and Alexa whirled round to see Giovanni emerging from the shadows of the room. 'I told him it was a dessert which tastes like an ice lolly.'

Her heart skipped, a beat and then began pounding as if it had only just learned how to. He looked like some dark, sensual predator, and Alexa hated the instinctive prickle of her skin and the tingling of her nerve-endings as her body instinctively acknowledged his. Because he was the father of her child—was *that* why she felt this bond which was almost tangible?

'Papà!' squealed Paolo in delight, as he extricated himself from her arms and jumped down, rushing over to Giovanni to attach himself with all the easy confidence of young puppy.

Papà? thought Alexa weakly. Already? When the hell had *that* happened?

Giovanni reached down to rumple the dark curls, and smiled. 'Did you drink lots of water? Because it's hot, and because—'

'*Water makes lions strong*!' put in Paolo enthusiastically, and went running back out onto the terrace as if he had lived in a palace all his life.

The unfamiliar expression threw her, and Alexa wondered what else Giovanni had managed to teach him in such a short space of time. That Italy was a much warmer and more hospitable climate than England? Or had Giovanni dangled the carrot of his wealth—telling Paolo that he owned a turquoise rectangle of a swimming pool which was as big as their local lido. And more. Much, much more.

'How quickly you have influenced him,' she said softly.

'Can you blame me?' Giovanni's mouth curved into a cruel line. 'I have four years' catching up to do.'

Face your fears, she told herself. Face them head-on. 'Are you working towards getting full custody of him, Giovanni? Is that what I'm fighting against?'

'Whoever said anything about fighting?' The sight of her—all bathed and fresh and sweetly scented—had just begun to register on his senses. 'That's the very last thing on my mind at the moment,' he murmured huskily, his black eyes sliding over her in a look of pure sexual scrutiny. 'How perfect you look, *cara.*'

Alexa sucked in a breath, trying to claw in enough oxygen so that she wouldn't do something unforgivable—like crumpling to the ground in front of him. Because that look was sheer, sizzling temptation. And because beneath the delicate silk of her new and unfamiliar robes she felt curiously naked. She felt the sudden melt of longing—was terrified that he might be able to detect from the subtle perfume of heightened sexual desire how much she wanted him. Through dry lips, she swallowed. 'Giovanni…'

He raised arrogant black brows. 'What?'

'Your son is out on the terrace,' she whispered, alarmed.

'So?'

'So stop trying to be provocative. He might see us.'

'What do you think most married couples do?' he demanded softly. 'They send silent messages with their eyes, and they whisper just what they plan to do when their child is safely tucked up in bed.'

It was both a warning and an invitation.

'But we're not married. Not properly.'

'Improperly, then. And maybe that's better. Marriage complicates things with emotions—this way we are free from such constraints. We can just enjoy the sex for what it is.' *Just as I originally intended*, he thought. Deliberately, he ran his tongue over his lips, and watched her eyes following the movement with a greed she could not hide, no matter how much she wanted to. 'Want me to do that to you, *cara mia*?'

'No.'

'Liar.'

He was right, damn him—but that didn't mean she was going to give in to what she really wanted. 'Please don't do this, Gio.'

He smiled. But it was a cruel, hard smile. Let her squirm. Let her plead. And then later let her gasp his name out loud in a different kind of plea altogether. 'I am not doing anything other than looking at you.'

How could she tell him that his looking at her was enough to set off a whole series of complex reactions to him—both physical and psychological? That the blaze of his ebony stare was making her turn to mush, drying her mouth to dust and making her knees shake? And her heart was hurting, as if he had taken a long sabre and stabbed it right through, because she could see the naked hostility which shone through his heavy-lidded desire.

Alexa opened her mouth to protest, but no words came. She felt as helpless as a newborn. He took advantage of her momentary weakness, snaking his hand out to capture her waist and pull her into his body.

It was an arrogant gesture of ownership which he had demonstrated many times with many women over the years. But this was different. Against her hair, Giovanni briefly closed his eyes, uncharacteristically weakened, just for a moment. It felt different. Because it *was* ownership? Because she was his wife, who had borne him a son? Yet she had cleverly run away and built herself a life without him—she who should have been closest to him was in fact a million miles away. But not for very much longer.

With the fingers of his free hand Giovanni jerked her chin up, so that her face was staring directly at him— the pale green eyes wary, the full lips trembling under his burning scrutiny.

'But you are right,' he conceded huskily. 'This is neither the time nor the place for love. Our son, as you reminded me, is out there on the terrace, and I must go to meet with Xavier, my half-brother.'

His mouth hardened. From being a man who had considered himself all alone in the world—it now seemed that he had relatives. He had already decided to make his claim on Alexa for Paolo—but how would having a half-brother impact on him? Would his sudden new royal status bring any influence to bear on his life? He forced himself to concentrate on that which he could control, and as he felt the distracting soft silk of her skin beneath his fingers he felt the sudden urgent leap of hunger. 'Have you seen the sleeping arrangements yet?'

'I'm afraid I have.' Turning her head, she wrenched her face away from his touch, from all the dangerous messages it was sending skittering along her skin.

'It will be quite like old times to share a bed, will it not, Alexa *mia*?' His smile was one of mocking triumph as he sensed her obvious discomfiture—enjoying the fact that she was fighting her feelings and trying to suppress her own desire. 'I, for one, cannot wait.'

'Well, I can—and I will. 'She drew a deep breath, knowing that this needed to be said. 'It doesn't matter how you've plotted or planned or connived to put us in the same bed—proximity means nothing in the face of my own determination. You won't have me, Giovanni— it would only complicate things,' she vowed softly, and she turned to walk outside.

Giovanni began to laugh softly as he watched her moving towards the terrace, seeing the pert thrust of her buttocks pushing against the fine, filmy fabric of her robe. How pointless her protest! How wasted her words!

Soon he would possess her in the most fundamental way possible. But this time he would use his prowess as a lover to tie her irrevocably to him.

When they had been married the stakes had been much lower. His pride had been badly hurt when she had left him—but in the end all he had lost had been a lying bride.

But with the discovery of Paolo everything had changed.

Alexa would never be allowed to run away from him again—because what she possessed was too valuable. She had something he wanted.

Their son.

And Giovanni was never going to lose him again.

CHAPTER EIGHT

ALEXA dressed for dinner with a cold feeling of dread at the pit of her stomach. How ironic that she found herself in a state which many women would find enviable—dining in a royal palace—and yet inside she was a bag of nerves.

But it wasn't etiquette which was bothering her—the fear that she might not curtsey to the right person, or might inadvertently use the wrong knife at dinner, or eat something she wasn't supposed to, or not want to eat something she *was* supposed to. No, she was worried about Giovanni—about what schemes were simmering away behind that implacable dark mask of a face.

And she was worried about her own unpredictable and volatile emotions. It was one thing to keep telling herself that he was the wrong man, but that didn't stop her heart racing when he was near. Or the stupid, sense-less longing to have him hold her, and look at her—with that melting look softening his hard black eyes—the way he'd once done such a long time ago. But—let's face it—he wasn't about to do that again, was he?

She felt as if she was in one of those subtle psychological thrillers, knowing that he was playing on her weakness and his strength. On the fact that a fiercely strong sexual attraction still burned between them. Even when they had been living together, and he had taunted her and despised her supposedly louche morals, he had still known exactly how to please her—even though his own particular brand of sexuality had been like making love to a man with no heart.

'Are you ready, *cara mia*?'

Just the sound of that soft Italian accent was enough to send whispers of awareness shivering all the way up her spine. Alexa looked up to see Giovanni standing at the door of Paolo's bedroom. She had been doing up the last button of Paolo's long silk tunic, worn with matching trousers, which their son had been given to wear by Sorrel. It had been a bit of a battle to persuade him to put them on, until Giovanni had reassured him that he, too, would be wearing traditional Kharastani dress for the evening meal.

'Why?' Paolo had wanted to know.

'Because it is courteous,' Giovanni had replied solemnly. 'And because surely you would like to look like a little prince for the night?'

That had swung it as far as Paolo was concerned, and Alexa's worries about how looking like a little prince might turn the child's head were instantly forgotten now, at the sight of Giovanni himself in the promised Kharastani costume.

He wore a robe of the finest silk she had ever seen,

coloured a deep sunset-red which made him look like a moving flame. A headdress in pure gold, held in place with a knotted scarlet circlet, completed the outfit. Alexa guessed that some men—if they carried a little extra weight, perhaps—might be in danger of looking ridiculous. But the way that the fabric flowed over Giovanni's hard and muscular body—he looked like a shimmering study in masculinity.

'Papà!' squealed Paolo. 'Do I look like a prince?'

'You look like a bold warrior,' Giovanni replied gravely.

'*Do* I?'

'Indeed you do. Now, come along—for we must not be late for dinner.'

Paolo rushed past him, and Alexa had no choice but to follow. But Giovanni did not move, just continued to stand in the doorway, as if he'd been fashioned from some hard, pure steel. She could feel the shivering of her skin beneath her gown.

'Let's go,' he said huskily, tearing his eyes away from the sudden thrusting points of her nipples against the fine silk of her gown. If only he were not constrained by palace rules and their child—he would be pinioning her up against the wall and thrusting into her.

The formal banquet for heads of state and visiting dignitaries had been held the night before—but this, the pre-wedding dinner, was a 'family' affair. It was held in a dining room which Malik had described as 'intimate'—but which was the size of a small ballroom, lined with gold and mirrors and priceless paintings.

The table was round, and set lavishly with crystal and

silver, and bowls full of richly scented roses. Tall white candles guttered and cast intriguing shadows, while robed figures slipped silently in and out of the room, carrying dishes which catered to the diners' every whim. In one corner was a small group of musicians who plucked on strangely shaped instruments to produce a sweet keening sound which was oddly haunting.

There were seven of them in total. As well as Alexa, Giovanni and Paolo sat Malik, with Sorrel close by. Next to her was Xavier, with Laura—his English fiancée.

'We don't usually eat this early,' said Malik, his hard black eyes momentarily crinkling in a smile down at Paolo. 'But then we are not usually honoured with such important guests as young Paolo.'

'But I can stay up late!' boasted Paolo, and followed this with an enormous yawn, which made everyone laugh.

Putting his heavy silver goblet down, Giovanni looked around the table, thinking what a disparate group they made. And that Malik seemed to be acting as host tonight, despite the presence of the royal groom.

Giovanni's eyes narrowed with curiosity. Perhaps Malik had taken over because Xavier and his fiancée were at that stage of being so much in love that they could barely tear their eyes away from each other.

Even today, when he and his half-brother had met in an attempt to piece together their patchy pasts, to see if they had anything in common, Xavier had been keen to get back to the woman who tomorrow he would make his wife.

Giovanni watched while the Frenchman poured water for her, touched his hand to her hair almost in wonder, and mirrored her body language in a way which would have pleased the most critical of behavioural psychologists.

His mouth twisted into a cynical smile. Had he ever felt like that about Alexa? He tried to think back, but his memories were tainted with bitterness and a sudden sobering dose of insight—that all of them were subject to the capricious whims of their hormones.

Love was just a word used by society to regularise a much more basic instinct—nature's imperative to continue the human race. What Xavier and Laura were experiencing right now was just a heightened state of sexual awareness—coupled with a compatibility which might or might not last. It probably wouldn't—if you took the time to study all the statistics. And marriages of mixed race fared even less well. His mouth hardened into an implacable line as he stared across the table at his deceitful wife. Just look what had happened to him and Alexa.

Did she feel his eyes on her? Was why she looked up and their gazes locked? Yet for a moment he felt a victim of the tricks that time sometimes played, losing himself in the softness of her green gaze, seeing a fleeting sadness there which briefly weighed heavy on his heart.

He saw her bite her lip as she turned her face away, the movement making her lush breasts move beneath the fine fabric of her tunic, and he had to swallow down his frustration as he felt the springing of his erection. How dared she affect that sad, almost mistreated air? She who had taken it upon herself to deny him his son!

Dampening down his anger, he turned instead to

speak to Malik—who seemed to be having some kind of uncomfortable exchange with the sassy blonde they called Sorrel. She was Malik's ward, and acted as if she was part of the family.

'The Sheikh will not be joining us for dinner?' Giovanni asked softly.

Malik shook his head. 'Unfortunately, no. These days, His Imperial Highness retires early—but he wishes to meet with you and Paolo tomorrow, before the wedding takes place.' Malik paused. 'And your wife, of course.'

Giovanni pondered this for a moment, hearing the unspoken question in the other man's words. He had not actually confirmed to Malik or anybody else that he and Alexa had long been estranged, though he suspected that it was common knowledge. He wasn't naïve enough to think that they would have admitted him to the close confines of the royal circle without having him thoroughly investigated—indeed, they probably knew everything about him, right down to his shoe-size. 'I see.'

'You are a man of few words,' Malik noted, raising his dark brows in query.

Giovanni smiled. He approved of a world where protocol forbade the asking of direct questions; a world where feelings could be acceptably buried and forgotten. 'I believe in keeping my own counsel,' he said softly.

Malik nodded. 'A wise strategy, for that is the Kharastani way—particularly for its royal men,' he observed sagely. 'I trust that you find your rooms adequate?' he added.

Giovanni smiled as their eyes met. How perfect! A

polite question about accommodation which disguised the real question underneath. 'More than adequate,' he murmured, and the eyes of the two men met in a moment of unspoken understanding.

Alexa heard the exchange between the two men, and her head jerked up in indignation as Giovanni spoke.

More than adequate? What would the select assembled group say if she suddenly blurted out that, no, they were *not* adequate—that in fact they were quite the opposite? That she had been put in a room and was expected to share it and a bed with her estranged husband, and she wasn't sure how she would be able to resist him?

But she knew how to behave at a royal banquet—or rather, how *not* to behave—and her generous hosts would learn nothing of her inner disquiet. Instead, she smiled at Laura. 'Are you nervous about the wedding?'

Laura shot a look at Xavier—but he was busy recounting a story to Giovanni about one of the Sheikh's famous racehorses, and not paying the two of them any attention. She bit her lip with an excitement which was almost palpable.

'I *should* be nervous,' she confided to Alexa. 'What with just about every royal family in the world being represented—not to mention all the politicians and filmstars, and the fact that I'm going to be photographed from just about every angle, and I'm terrified I've got a spot brewing—but the thing is…' Her voice tailed off and her eyes grew misty and dreamy. 'I love Xavier so much that none of it seems to matter—we could be standing barefoot on a deserted beach, for all I care!'

'*Fantastique!*' interjected Xavier silkily, who had clearly heard the last part of the sentence. He shot Alexa a mischievous look. 'They are calling it the wedding of the decade, and yet now I realise that we could have eloped to the Maldives for all Laura cares!'

'Because it's *you* I'm marrying!' pouted Laura. 'And you're the only important person.'

'Am I, now, *cherie*?' he questioned softly.

Their love was incandescent, and Alexa was glad of their glowing happiness, but it was hard not to feel a twinge of envy. She remembered her own engagement. That had been equally ecstatic. But she could see now that all their idealistic expectations had made it seem unreal—as different from Xavier and Laura's easy familiarity as chalk was to cheese.

Giovanni had behaved with almost exaggerated regard for her, and Alexa had let him, not having the self-confidence to do anything other than accede to his wishes. She had been so in love—and so disbelieving of the fact that he seemed to feel the same way—that she honestly thought she would have dyed her hair green and walked on burning coals if he'd asked her to. *Or let him believe you were a virgin by implication?* an inner voice questioned painfully. Alexa winced. How could anything so unequal ever have lasted the course?

But she did her best to put such futile introspection out of her mind, and to concentrate on an experience she was unlikely to repeat once the wedding celebrations were over. Dinner in a palace!

Course after course was placed before them. Meats and fruits and figs and pastries—and a huge fish which had been cooked with raisins, carried in by two people on an enormous golden platter.

Alexa thought that Paolo had behaved extremely well during the protracted feast—every adult around the table had been paying him lots of attention and he had revelled in it—but when he demanded a grape and added, somewhat imperiously, "And you must peel it for me, Mamma!" she knew it was time for a reality check.

'I think you've had enough to eat, darling,' she said gently. 'And I think it's time I took you to bed—it's been a long day.'

'*I don't wanna go to bed!*'

Alexa winced, guessing that this rare tantrum had been long overdue in light of the dizzying array of events which had taken place—but that didn't stop her cheeks from burning with embarrassment as she scrambled to her feet, wondering if Giovanni would try to cite this untoward scene as an example of her poor mothering skills.

Yet when Giovanni looked up there was no expression of recrimination on his face, though his black eyes remained enigmatic. 'You want me to come and help?'

Such a simple question—yet it had the power to tug unbearably at her heartstrings. Because it was just the kind of thing a normal husband might have asked his wife and Alexa could have wept for what might have been. Theirs wasn't a *normal* relationship, she reminded herself fiercely—it never had been and it never could be. And Giovanni wasn't stupid—on the contrary, he was an operator *par excellence*. His remark had probably only come out as being caring and solicitous because they were in company, and he was aware that the others were watching, listening.

How much *did* the others know about their situation—how much had he told them? Had he painted her as the hard-hearted bitch of some of his more heated accusations? But, if so, then Xavier and the others were showing no sign of disapproval. On the contrary, she had been shown nothing but consideration and courtesy by everyone here this evening, and it made her feel pensive. How she would have loved to be a proper part of a group like this—feeling she belonged somewhere.

Giovanni's black eyes were still trained on her in glittering question, but Alexa shook her head.

'No, honestly—I'm fine on my own, thanks. Goodnight, everyone.'

'You look tired,' said Laura, frowning.

'I am. Completely bushed,' admitted Alexa.

Maybe Giovanni would take the hint, she thought—more with hope than conviction. Maybe he would sit up late, talking and drinking with Xavier and Malik—and by the time he came to bed he would find her sound asleep and leave her alone.

Maybe.

A servant was there to guide her through the cool marbled corridors back to their suite, and in an effort to quell the relentless chatter in her head Alexa forced herself to concentrate on the small things while she got Paolo ready for bed. The wash of moonlight on the floor. The heavy scent of roses in a gleaming vase. The trace of jasmine as it floated in through the open shutters on a gentle breeze. What a beautiful place this was, she thought wistfully as she squeezed a blob of toothpaste onto Paolo's brush.

She lit a couple of low lamps, and Paolo was so exhausted that he was almost asleep by the time she pulled the cotton sheet over him. None of her fears about him being freaked out by such strange, new surroundings were fulfilled.

Hadn't there been a part of her which had hoped he might be a little fractious and unsettled, causing her to have to stay with him in a kind of motherly vigil?

Lovingly, she stared down at the dark lashes which formed two soft arcs, brushing against his olive skin. Oh, Paolo, she thought.

'Night, Mamma,' he murmured sleepily.

'Night-night, darling—sleep tight.' But his breathing had already settled into a soft, deep rhythm.

So now what did she do?

There really wasn't a lot of choice open to her. She did not want to sleep with her husband, that was for sure. Far too dangerous—on so many different levels. But she was equally certain that Giovanni wouldn't dream of camping out on one of those low divans in the sitting room—which meant that she would have to. He could have the huge bed to himself and get on with it!

Quickly she undressed, and took out a long night-gown which Teri had insisted on giving her for the trip, along with two matching bra and knickers sets.

'Nightwear and lingerie can *never* be done on the cheap,' her boss had said, and when Alexa had shaken her head in protest, she had added firmly. 'Take them, Lex—and look on it as a bonus for being such a good worker.'

Wasn't there a part of every woman which adored luxury? Alexa hadn't needed asking twice. With its soft layers of oyster silk-satin and lace, the gown felt like heaven—but at least it swept the ground in a relatively demure way. So if she needed to get up in the middle of the night, then at least Giovanni wouldn't be able to accuse her of provocation.

Brushing her long hair so that it spilled in a golden waterfall all the way down her back, she took a pillow and a heavy satin coverlet from the four-poster bed and made herself a makeshift bed on a divan, then climbed into it and prayed for the solace of sleep.

Outside, she could hear the sound of some unknown bird calling in the palace gardens—was that the Kharastani equivalent of an owl? she wondered sleepily. Moonlight crept in through the slatted shutters, reliev-ing the darkness with muted silver stripes of light. The divan wasn't soft, and the one pillow was woefully in-adequate—but maybe the emotional maelstrom of the last few days had been enough to completely exhaust her because, almost with a sense of disbelief, Alexa quickly felt herself sinking into the dark embrace of slumber.

But if she slept then she had no recollection of it—

because it seemed almost as soon as her eyelids had
drifted wearily down she was startled by a soft sound
in the room, and her eyes fluttered drowsily open.

Which of her senses was engaged first?

Was it his presence she felt, or did she hear the sound
of his breathing?

Or was it the gradual readjustment of her eyes to the
flickering light which began to register on her consciousness? Giovanni was standing by the divan, a beau-
tifully intricate silver lamp in his hand.

For a moment she thought she must be dreaming as her
eyes made the visual connection before her brain had
time to decipher all the implications of his presence. His
torso was bare, and around his waist was knotted a long
piece of material which gleamed golden and scarlet in the
lamplight. He had told his son that he looked like a warrior
king, but in that moment he looked like a king himself.

Almost in slow motion, she watched him put the
lamp down and then unknot the heavy gold brocade at
his hip, so that it fell to his feet with a heavy sigh.

And suddenly he was naked.

He stood there, dark and haughty, comfortable and
unashamed by his nakedness—and who could blame
him? The glimmering light emphasised the long, tawny
limbs, the broad, hard chest and flat belly. He really was
the most perfect example of the male of the species, she
thought, with an aching sense of longing.

Unwillingly, but irresistibly, her eyes travelled
slowly down his body- to the very fork of his masculinity. Amid the coiled dark forest of hair was the paler

hint of his manhood, and Alexa found her lips drying, knowing that she should feel appalled at the sudden longing which caught her by the throat and by the heart. *Was* she dreaming?

'Giovanni.' She swallowed.

Carefully, he sat on the edge of the divan—close enough for the animal warmth of his body to radiate its heat, but not close enough to threaten her. In the soft lamplight, she lay back, her eyes wide and dark and her face a pale blur. But it was her hair which captivated him—all red-gold satin which spilled out over the pillows around her. That and the dark petals of her lips which had parted in unconscious invitation.

'You were sleeping,' he said, but there was a sudden and unexpected lump in his throat.

What was it? The softness of his voice which lulled her, or the building ache of hunger which threatened to silence her every objection?

'I feel like I still am,' she said, and part of her wanted him to destroy this spell that the darkness had woven around them. To make her safe to reject him. To *want* to reject him.

'Why are you in here, Lex?' he murmured. 'All alone on this hard and unforgiving divan?'

'You know…you know why,' she said, hating her hesitancy—the stammering uncertainty of her response—and the hunger to have him touch her even though every fibre of her being told her unequivocally that it would be wrong.

'No, I don't.'

'Giovanni…'

'What is it?'

'I—'

'*Bella*,' he murmured. '*Bella mia.*'

His words were cajoling, coaxing—seeming to beg all kinds of confidences. But she dared not begin to speak, for fear that she would blurt out just how beautiful he was. And how much she had missed seeing his hard dark and golden body naked like this. How the absence of the intimacy of marriage could leave you bereft—even if that marriage had not been one which was made in heaven.

He wondered if she was aware that her nipples had begun to peak through the fine material of her nightgown. That the soft silk clung to her thighs, skated over the flat plane of her belly and skimmed over the narrow curve of her hips. Had ever a woman both tantalised and disappointed him as much as Alexa?

Dio, but he wanted her!

Reaching out, he placed the tip of his thumb beneath her chin, rubbing it in a slow, enticing movement, tempering his hunger with careful, unthreatening seduction. 'You're tense,' he murmured, as the thumb slid along the curve of her jaw. 'Relax.'

Relax? When just the touch of him was beginning to scramble her senses? How long had it been since a naked man had stroked her skin in the middle of the night like this? All her reasons for being kept awake in recent years had been of a far more practical nature.

She remembered the sleepless nights of Paolo's

childhood fevers. The mopping of his hot brow and the sharp tear of panic and fright—until the crisis had passed and the pale light of morning had crept in.

She remembered too the time when there had been no permanent job—before Teri had opened the shop in the village—and the worry about how she was going to support the two of them without the indignity of having to ask the State for support.

Her mother was living so far away that she might as well be residing on a distant planet—and she had made it very clear that she thought Alexa was a fool to have ended up as a single mother with no alimony. There had been no one to ask and no one to share her growing dread, and during that time Alexa had learnt the harsh definition of how it felt to be completely on her own.

Did the barren quality of her life since Giovanni explain why she was lying there now, as compliant as a cat being stroked by its master?

Alexa tipped her head back, and her protest seemed to be torn reluctantly from between dry lips. 'Leave it, Gio. Please.'

But she might as well not have spoken, for he did not heed her words, nor loosen his hold on her, just continued to stroke reflectively at her flesh as if he had all the time in the world.

And how was it that even a touch as innocuous as that could weave such a powerfully sensual spell, sending whispering little messages of need and desire skittering over her skin? Alexa could feel the sudden acceleration of her heart, the heated flush to her face as he arrogantly moved his hand down to cup her engorged breast, and she looked at him, startled, even while the nipple sprang harder still into pert life beneath his questing fingers.

'You want me,' he whispered. 'You want me, *cara mia*. You always did and you always will.'

It was an outrageous sexual boast, and Alexa wanted to deny him—to deny to herself the fundamental truth contained within it—but the expert caress of his fingers was making her melt beneath him.

'Gio…'

Her eyelids fluttered to a close, and Giovanni allowed himself a small smile of triumph as he bent his dark head and began to kiss her, his mouth grazing hers, feeling her lips part and the warmth of her breath as it mingled with his.

'Don't you?' he persisted, his voice muffled against the sweet taste of her skin.

The pressure of his lips stopped her from replying— or was she simply fooling herself? Because from where could she summon up the strength to tell him to stop what he was doing when it felt as if she had been fast-tracked into paradise? And now he was moving his hand down, so that it lay on the flat of her belly, circling there reflectively. For a moment Alexa froze, waiting for some kind of recrimination—as if he would suddenly start berating her for what that belly had carried within it without his knowledge.

But he made no such accusation. Instead, he drifted his fingers downwards, over the slippery silk, and then further still—heading inexorably but with agonising slowness towards the centre of longing at the fork of her thighs.

'Don't you?' he said again, drawing his mouth away from her by a fraction as he felt her body stiffen in anticipation.

Alexa swallowed. In the dim half-light she could see the feverish glitter of his eyes, and she lifted her hand to touch the hard contours of his face with its fierce look of intent. She could say no, that she didn't want him—but wouldn't that be one more lie to add to the pile? And in a way wasn't this inevitable? Hadn't it been inevitable since he'd walked into the shop and back into her life last week? 'Yes,' she admitted brokenly. 'Yes, I want you.'

Giovanni knew then that he had her—and that he could make her beg for him if he so desired. Yet if this was victory, it seemed a hollow one—and for once in his life he wasn't sure why.

His mouth hardened, for confusion was an emotion he could do without. 'Come. We must not wake our son,' he said, and he bent to lift her into his arms, holding her up against his bare chest.

Was Alexa imagining the sudden disapproval colouring his voice? She must have been—because why else would he be stroking his fingers teasingly over the silk-covered globe of her bottom as he carried her through to the master bedroom? Yet, although his hands were gentle, his face was implacable as he carried her into the bedroom and laid her down on the bed.

For a moment he just stood, towering over her, staring at her with an expression she had never seen on

his face before. Then with a cruel smile he reached
down, catching hold of the delicate fabric with both
hands and tearing it apart with a single wrench to lay
bare her pale and beautiful body.

Alexa gasped as she heard it rip, and felt warm,
scented air rushing onto her bare skin.

'What did you do that for?'

He did not know. To destroy something which was
hers? Or to remind himself that ultimately everything
was disposable? Silk-satin was no different from the
vows made during a marriage ceremony—they could
both be torn to shreds. 'Let's just say I couldn't wait,'
he said, in a dangerous voice.

Alexa knew she should have protested—told him
that he had just destroyed an expensive gift which might
not mean much to him, but sure as hell meant a lot to
her. But it was too late for that. Too late to do anything
other than gasp again—only this time with pleasure. For
he had begun to kiss her again, and his warm naked form
was lowering itself on top of her—it seemed that he had
spoken the truth and that he couldn't wait. Or didn't
want to. Because he was big, and hard, and—oh,
heavens—now he was stroking on a condom.

'Gio!' she gasped.

Hard, honed flesh was melding with the soft, giving
nature of hers. His hand was between her legs—fingers
luxuriating in her honeyed wetness—and she could feel
the tip of him nudging against her as he said something in
Italian that in her befuddled state she could not understand.

What was it that made her wrap her legs around his

back and push her hips up invitingly towards him—as if all the harsh words and bitterness between them had not happened? Was it simply a sexual hunger which had gone too long unfed? Or was it because deep down, in spite of everything, it was Giovanni who had dominated her waking thoughts and night-time dreams for so long, even though she had done everything in her power to try to forget him?

The man she had loved.

And loved still?

'No!' she whimpered in denial.

He stilled. 'No?' he drawled, in disbelief.

'Yes,' she whispered, and brushed her lips to his shoulder, her fingers tangling in the dark silky waves of his hair. 'I meant…yes.'

Perversely, her slurred words of incitement made him hold back. To show that *he* held all the power, and not her. To prove to himself that he could make her beg and make her wait while *he* had the self-will to resist the wanton thrust of her hips

But then she touched her lips to his throat, licking at the hollow there, the way she'd used to, and that one small gesture took him right back to a time when he had seen in her all his hopes and dreams of a glorious and golden future. For a split-second Giovanni felt as if she had ripped his chest open and was watching his raw heart pumping there.

Furiously he thrust into her, harder and deeper than he had ever thrust into a woman before, as he forced himself to forget that he had married her, that she had ever been more to him than she was at this moment. Just a perfect and willing body sharing his bed. She is *nothing* to you, he told himself fiercely, and shut his eyes to blot her out.

'Giovanni—'

'What?' he growled.

Alexa's fingers bit into his broad shoulders as he moved inside her, seeming to stab at her heart itself as he took her further and further towards the peak of glorious fulfilment. Yet somehow it seemed like an *empty* pleasure. Even as she felt the encroaching rush of desire lapping at the edges of consciousness she realised that he was no longer kissing her.

Above her, his face was a mask—his closed eyes were not seeing *her*—and even though his body moved with such sweet and piercing accuracy inside hers the whole act somehow felt *mechanical*.

He wasn't making love to her—he was having sex with her. Physically satisfying, but cold and functional sex.

She felt a silent anguished protest scream from deep within her, yet it was too late to back out now. Too late to halt the great building whoosh of pleasure. Her own body seemed like a traitor as it came to shivering completion in his arms.

Yet try as he might—in the dark, flowering moment of his own release -Giovanni could not shake off the thought that this *did* feel different. That he had once desired her in a way which had taken his breath away—and, even if you discounted that, his child had been nurtured within her womb in the interim. A part of *him* had grown inside *her*.

Unexpectedly, emotion ripped through him as a ragged cry was torn from his lips. He felt as if the universe was imploding behind his eyes. As if he might die at the very height of it—and that such a death would be matchless and perfect.

He had planned to distance himself afterwards, to roll away from her and to sleep on the other side of the vast bed until his desire returned once more and he could reach for her with nothing other than passion on his mind. But somehow it didn't happen. He couldn't move from where he lay, still locked inside her, with his dark head cradled on her breast as he felt the last of the blissful spasms dying away.

'Gio?' questioned Alexa, wondering just where the hell they were going after this. But her one-word question fell on ears that did not hear, and she blinked her eyes with something like surprise.

For Giovanni was already asleep.

CHAPTER NINE

ALEXA spent a fitful and apprehensive night while Giovanni slept beside her—the sheets rumpled beneath one hard, dark thigh while his hand rested carelessly at the dip in her waist.

She lay still as their naked bodies brushed together and her ripped nightgown lay in tatters on the floor, and wondered how she could have behaved in a way which was so horribly *predictable*.

It wasn't even as if she had been coerced into it. He hadn't brutally crushed her into his arms the way he'd done that time at her little house, when he'd gone all out to demonstrate his whole repertoire of sensual skills, had he? In fact, he had simply appeared by her bed and let his wrap flutter to the ground—like some cheesy stripper. And she had let him stroke her face and touch her breasts and then practically gone down on her hands and knees and begged him to make love to her.

Make love?

If it wouldn't have risked waking him then she would have let out an ironic laugh. She had placed herself in enough emotional danger without adding to it—and if she started imagining that what had happened between them last night had been *making love* then she would be in real jeopardy.

Resisting the urge to wriggle her body restlessly, for fear that it would disturb the virile form of the sleeping man beside her, Alexa stared at the patterns on the ceiling—at the shimmering movement of moonlight reflected through the crystal drops of the chandelier—as night-time drifted slowly into day.

What had she done?

She had compromised herself utterly and completely, that was what she had done. Had had loveless sex with a man who had made no secret of despising her—or of his macho view of the world and a woman's place in it. Wouldn't he despise her even more now? The easy virtue he had always accused her of—and which she had always hotly denied—would now seem to have been explicitly confirmed by her actions.

She wasn't stupid. She knew what he wanted—something which all his wealth and power could not buy him. His son. And if he went ahead with a legal battle to gain custody then what chance would she have? What kind of picture would he have his clever over-paid lawyers paint of her? A wanton? A slut? A *puttana*, as they said in Italy.

In the end, she went to sleep at the worst possible time—dozing off just before daybreak and thus having to abandon her plan to slip quietly from the bed and get showered and dressed in time to wake Paolo, and not risk him having to see…

'*Papà*! What are you doing here, Papà?'

Paolo's delighted little voice broke into the cloud of her disturbed dreams and Alexa opened her eyes in time to see her son's pyjama-clad figure hurtling towards the bed—where an indolently Giovanni lay like a watchful black panther against the bank of pillows.

'What does it look like?' Giovanni questioned indulgently as the child hurled himself at him, like a tiny steam train. He smiled as he held his arms out and cuddled the child to him, then yawned. 'Waking up.'

Paolo stared at him. 'Will you always sleep with Mamma now?'

Black eyes glittered from over the top of Paolo's head in Alexa's direction, but they were watchful, wary. Last night had shaken him. Had left him feeling a way he had not expected to feel. Light-headed, and not quite real. His voice hardened as he closed his mind to it. 'You will have to ask her that yourself.'

The look she returned to him simmered with an unspoken fury. She was hating her son having to witness her looking like this—with her bedhead hair. Paolo was used to seeing her in an oversized T-shirt, and her nakedness beneath the bedclothes made her feel vulnerable and defenceless—as well as diminishing her opportunities for flouncing out with her dignity intact.

She clutched the sheet to her chin with one hand and ruffled Paolo's dark curls with the other. 'Um, darling, would you mind passing Mamma the dressing gown I left lying over there on the chair?'

'Allow me,' interposed a silken voice.

And, to Alexa's horror, she saw Giovanni gracefully uncurl the child from his arms and get out of bed—completely naked himself—and saunter over to the satin kimono as if it was perfectly acceptable for him to pad around the place with nothing on.

Her eyes flashed a message at him. *Put some damned clothes on.*

He met the look and smiled, his eyes dilating by a fraction as he picked up the green gown and carried it over to her, subtly kicking her ripped nightgown out of sight, which made Alexa's cheeks flare with mortification. He had torn that expensive nightie from her body— and she had just *let* him!

'Paolo, why don't you go and brush your teeth and Mamma will come and find you in a minute?' Alexa suggested furiously, though she was trembling so much she was amazed that the sentence sounded coherent.

'Okay!'

She waited until he had run out of the room before she rounded on Giovanni. It was as much as she could do not to beat her fists on his chest—but she wasn't naïve enough to risk something as provocative as *that*. 'How dare you?' she breathed. 'How dare you?'

'What, in particular, are you objecting to?' he drawled.

'Parading around with *no clothes on*!' she choked.

'What's the matter—has he never seen a naked man before?'

'Of course he hasn't!'

'Ah!' He bit back a smile of unmistakable satisfaction. 'He hasn't?'

She had walked straight into a trick question, and Alexa glared at him. She knew it was perverse—but some misunderstood demon inside her wanted to tell him that, yes, Paolo had seen a thousand naked men pass through her bedroom. That she entertained lovers with all the unembarrassed ease of an ancient courtesan!

'Of course he hasn't!' she said again crossly. 'Not that you're likely to believe that, of course—you just believe what happens to suit you at the time, don't you, Giovanni? So therefore a woman who's not a virgin *must* be a slut—because there's never any room for grey in your world, is there? Only black and white! Always bending reality to suit your vision of it!'

He thought how magnificent she looked. How, if it weren't for a list of royal engagements and their young son waiting for them nearby, she would be writhing beneath him by now. Cursing the fact that he had slept right through the night without taking advantage of the opportunity for more sex with her, he spread the palms of his hands out in a gesture of admission. 'You may have a point,' he said softly.

Alexa stilled, not sure if she'd heard him properly. 'Let me get this straight. I no longer top your list of sexual predators? You're *agreeing* with me?' she questioned suspiciously.

Giovanni was astute enough to recognise that more accusation would work against him. Last night had been a one-off—an undeniably powerful coupling, driven by hurt and anger and bitter memories of the past as well as by sexual hunger. But in a way the act had been ca-

thartic—washing everything away—and if he wanted a
repeat performance, then he was going to have to
employ a completely different strategy towards her.

'I am saying that you have a point,' he conceded, as
careful with his words as any lawyer.

Once, the acknowledgement might have filled her with
a sense of victory—but it was far too late for that. It didn't
matter that he might have misjudged her and been harsh
on her—all that was irrelevant now, and only their son
counted. 'But all of that is completely beside the point.
What about Paolo walking in like that, to see—?'

'Two grown adults doing what comes completely
naturally?'

'Don't wilfully misunderstand me, Giovanni!' Alexa
clenched her fists. 'I can understand that you weren't
going to be satisfied until you got what you wanted—'

'Whereas you didn't want it at all, I suppose?' he
enquired sardonically. 'I really had to fight to get you
to submit to my wicked way, didn't I?'

She ignored the interruption and its wounding
accuracy. 'But you could have had the decency to creep
away before it got light and sleep on one of the divans. At
least that way Paolo wouldn't have had to witness—'

'To witness what? A husband and wife waking up in
bed together?' he queried silkily. 'You think that is such
a terrible crime, *cara*?'

'Yes, I do—in our case!' She darted a look towards
the bathroom door, but thankfully there was still no sign
of Paolo. Alexa pulled on the dark silk kimono and
knotted it tightly at her waist, raking her hand through

her tumble of hair and thinking what a sight she must look. 'We aren't even supposed to be married any more—just in case you'd forgotten!'

'I am having trouble remembering anything right now—especially with the golden silk of your hair tumbling down over your breasts like that,' he said huskily.

She would have had to be made of ice not to respond to the sensual compliment, and she had already proved beyond reasonable doubt that being glacial was not in her nature—not around Giovanni. Alexa drew in a deep breath. 'Can you *please* put some clothes on?'

He shot her a mocking look. 'That's the first time I've ever been asked *that* particular question.'

He walked into the bathroom and returned wearing a white towel knotted around his narrow hips, but even that could not disguise the unmistakable outline of his rapidly growing desire. He saw her eyes drawn to it convulsively, and then dart away again before they fixed themselves on his face. 'Frustrating, isn't it, *bella*?' he murmured.

'What the hell are we going to do?'

'About the frustration, or about the day's plans?'

'Gio!'

He touched his fingers to the rough rasp of new growth at his jaw, thinking that he needed a shave and feeling—uncharacteristically—that he was out of his depth. He was a man who considered that he knew all the rules of sexual behaviour—yet this was entirely new territory for him.

For a start, he didn't usually bed women who had children—not unless they were older and safely out of the way. In fact, he didn't involve himself with anything which threatened to cramp his style—and that included jealous husbands or mothers-on-the-make who wanted an assurance that he would marry their daughters if he happened to conduct an affair with them.

In all these matters he was obdurate and determined—never allowing himself to be swayed, no matter what the provocation. And if that was considered selfish, then so be it—at least Giovanni was honest; he never promised something he couldn't deliver. Pleasure without strings. If the woman didn't like it, then *duro*— tough—there was always another, just as beautiful, waiting to be given whatever Giovanni da Verrazzano was prepared to offer.

But with Alexa…the child in question was *their* child—and that put an entirely different perspective on the situation. He found he didn't *want* to demand coldly that she hire in a babysitter. He *wanted* to share breakfast with their son. Yet wouldn't admitting that show him as vulnerable—expose a side of himself which she might use against him in any future battle for their son?

His hard, dark face gave away nothing of his conflicting thoughts. 'We are presenting our son to the Sheikh, and then going to the wedding of Xavier and Laura, as planned.' He gave her an icy smile. 'Nothing has changed, *cara*—did you really expect it to?'

Alexa stared at him. 'Nothing?' She had asked him to stop making allusions to sex, but she had not expected all the vigour to suddenly drain from his face, leaving the eyes cold and the mouth cruel. 'Are you saying that last night isn't going to impact on us one way or another?' she questioned slowly.

He raised his dark brows. 'That is up to you,' he said. 'It can impact on us any time you like—you have only to say the word and we'll enjoy an action replay.' Black eyes danced a sensual message. 'Satisfaction guaranteed.'

'You arrogant—'

'But it's the truth,' he murmured sardonically. 'You know it and I know it.'

'*Bastard!*' she hissed.

'Keep your voice down, Lex—I don't want Paolo growing up around bad language.'

Rarely had Alexa felt so frustrated or so angry, but presumably that was his intention. Not trusting herself to reply and give him the satisfaction of knowing that, she turned on her heel and went to persuade Paolo to wear the outfit she'd brought for him.

He submitted fairly peacefully to her ministrations, and afterwards, while he was being served with fresh fruit and pastries on a terrace already warm from the sun—though it was not yet high in the sky—Alexa pulled out her own wedding outfit. She tried to be enthusiastic about the accessories which Teri had recommended to match the full-length sheath dress coloured an unusual shade of cobalt green.

Large dangly green earrings and a clutch of bangles clattering at her wrist brought the whole outfit together, and when she looked in the mirror it was with the satisfaction of knowing she looked her best. That the reflection which stared back at her was of a young and attractive woman in her prime—not a hard-up shop girl for whom every penny counted.

But above the unusual garb Alexa's face was drained, and she sighed. What on earth was she going to say to Giovanni's father, the Sheikh?

'Lex?' came a voice from behind her.

She turned round to see Giovanni, looking as if he was born to live in a palace—his dark skin and black eyes standing out in stark relief against the pale, fluid robes he wore.

'What's up?' he asked.

Like he *cared*! 'Oh, you know.' Affecting nonchalance, she shrugged. 'Someone should write an etiquette book along the lines of: *How To Cope When the Father of Your Child Announces He's Royal*!' And, of course, the follow-up volume: *Meeting His Father For the First Time*!

The merest glimmer of a smile curved the corners of a mouth more habitually seen set in a forbidding line. 'You're nervous?'

'What do you think? That I meet sheikhs every day of the week?'

'I think you look beautiful and that you are a good mother. That's what I think,' he said unexpectedly.

The compliment took her by surprise, and warmed her far more than it should have done. Was that because he hadn't paid her one for such a long time? She blushed, and then hated herself for blushing. *Just because he's stopped being nasty to you for a split second, it doesn't mean you should read anything into it.*

She stared instead at his white robes and headdress,

the purity of the garments broken only by the splash of colour on his headdress and sash. 'I thought only the bride was supposed to wear white.'

'Not in Kharastan. Apparently she's in red and gold—lavish embroidery and lots of jewels. Are you and Paolo ready to see Zahir now?'

Alexa knew she couldn't put it off for ever.

'Yes,' she answered quietly.

'And have you told Paolo?'

Again, she nodded. 'I have.' Her expression was wry. 'If there's one thing I've learnt from all this, it's that total honesty is best where children are concerned.'

'Only children?' he mocked softly. 'You mean that lies are acceptable when you're dealing with adults?'

She looked at him, wondering how the face she had touched with such rapture under the concealing darkness of the night should now seem so distant and remote. 'I'll never lie to you again, Giovanni,' she vowed.

He turned away. Words were so easy. They could be plucked from out of nowhere at will. And he had no need of her reassurances. 'Let us go and find our son,' he said harshly, hardening his heart against the faint look of disappointment on her face.

The three of them went off to the Sheikh's private quarters. The rooms were large and cool, and there were treasures here more stunning than anything else she'd seen in the palace, but in a way Alexa was oblivious to everything other than the significance of the occasion.

The Sheikh was very old, and was seated on a beautiful cushion-scattered seat by a window overlooking a rose garden. He beckoned to them to approach. Paolo's hand slipped quietly into hers, and when they grew closer Alexa surprised herself by dropping a deep curtsey she hadn't been aware she knew how to do.

'Please.' The Sheikh smiled and patted the space on the divan beside him as he looked at the boy. 'Do you want to sit down beside me?' he asked Paolo.

To Alexa's astonishment, Paolo went immediately, hopping up easily and swinging his little legs as if he was sitting on the wall outside school! Was that because he had been starved of extended family from the word go? Only a grandmother in Canada whom he saw maybe once every couple of years, if he was lucky?

For a moment she felt stricken with a heavy kind of guilt and turned her head to see Giovanni's gaze, expecting to find accusation firing from his black eyes. But, no. Instead, she was startled by a brief glimmer of admiration in their ebony depths—or was she imagining it? But no, he had told her that he thought her a good mother, and there was no reason for him to tell lies about that—especially not when he had been so brutally honest about everything else.

The Sheikh began to talk softly to Paolo, telling him about what it had been like growing up in Kharastan, and Alexa thought that the tale was as much for his son as his grandson. He talked about the desert, where flowers bloomed only once in a century and where camels walked for unimaginable amounts of time, and he described the ancient art of keeping falcons—the wild, savage beauty of these birds of prey. With an expression of unmistakable pride, he described the fine racehorses he kept in his stables. 'Do you ride, Paolo?'

'No, sir.'

'Would you like to?'

'Oh, yes, please, sir!'

Afterwards, they all took sweet mint tea and the ordeal was nothing remotely as terrifying as Alexa had feared. But when they were about to leave, the Sheikh summoned for her to remain behind.

She looked beseechingly at Giovanni, but his black eyes glittered unperturbed as he placed his hand on Paolo's shoulder.

'Want to go and see all the acrobats practising?'

'*Acrobats?*' squeaked Paolo.

The Sheikh gave a smile. 'Indeed, there are acrobats,' he said gravely. 'And magicians, musicians and dancers—for in Kharastan a royal wedding is rare, and something to be truly celebrated!'

After they'd gone, there was silence for a moment. Alexa wasn't experienced in handling royals, but she knew that you were never supposed to initiate conversation—especially so in a country where it seemed that women were submissive. Remembering something else she had read, she dropped her gaze so that her eyes were downcast.

'You have a fine boy,' said the Sheikh at last.

His words made her look up and, inspired by surprise as much as relief, Alexa's face broke into a wreath of a smile. 'Why, thank you.'

The Sheikh nodded, and there was a pause. 'But he has had a hard life, I understand?'

Alexa stilled. 'Hard? I'm not sure that I understand, your Imperial Highness.'

'Giovanni tells me that you live in a small cottage and that you work in a shop.'

Oh, did he? Never considered particularly tall, Alexa now instinctively drew herself up to her full height, and sucked in a breath of angry air through her nostrils. 'We may not have much in the material sense,' she said, with quiet dignity, 'but Paolo has never gone short on the things that matter. He's always had sustenance, play and comfort—but more importantly than anything he's always had love. An abundance of love. So I don't think his life has been at all hard, Your Highness—I must disagree with your son.'

The Sheikh's eyes narrowed with a glint of humour. 'From what I understand, there are many disagreements between the two of you—but your relationship with Giovanni is not my concern. My grandson, however, is. The sentiment that money cannot not buy love has always been true—but money *can* buy you comfort,' he said.

'It can buy *material* comfort,' Alexa emphasised. 'Emotional comfort is far more elusive.'

'Only women place importance on such things,' he said dismissively.

But Alexa was not one of his servants—there to be banished because her views didn't happen to coincide with his. Yes, he was all-powerful within his kingdom— but surely it was morally wrong to agree with him just because of that?

'Women are usually the ones left caring for the family,' she argued. 'And we recognise the importance of emotion.'

He stared at her. 'You are stubborn,' he said suddenly.

'No. I'm passionate about the things I believe in, Your Majesty.'

'We sometimes have to live without the things we believe in,' he said softly, and then shut his eyes and leaned back, suddenly weary. 'Thank you for talking to me. Now, go and enjoy the wedding.'

Was he sending her a silent message? Telling her that she was *wasting her time* if she was hoping for a show of emotion from Giovanni? Well, you needn't worry, Your Imperial Highness, she thought—I'm under no illusions where Giovanni is concerned.

A servant took her to where Paolo was standing, down in the courtyard, being given a private performance by a set of jugglers. Giovanni was standing a short distance away, beside an orange tree which bore both fruit and flower.

He looked up with a questioning stare as she approached. 'Your meeting with the Sheikh went well?'

'Surprisingly well, considering.'

'Considering what?' His voice was cool.

Alexa narrowed her eyes. 'Did you describe Paolo's life as hard?'

There was a pause. 'Of course.'

Count to ten. Keep calm. Don't lose it. But it wasn't easy when she wanted to scream her outrage to the rooftops. 'How could you say that? It's not *hard*,' she defended breathlessly. 'Your son is loved and wanted. Even the Sheikh acknowledged that much.'

'My son does not have a father,' he said coldly. 'Nor all the advantages that my wealth could bring him—'

'But—'

'Hear me out, Alexa!' His words cut through her objections like a knife through a ripe peach. 'I had not intended to bring this up until after the wedding, but since you seem determined to have the discussion I have no choice.'

'Choice? What are you talking about?'

'Considering all the odds which have been stacked against Paolo—'

'What *odds*?' she questioned, in a dangerous voice.

'The fact that you are a single working mother and that you cannot afford to buy your own home.' He saw her look of objection and shook his dark head. 'These are not things that I am simply *making up*, *cara*,' he intoned fiercely. 'They are known obstacles to a child's proper development. You know that. I know that.'

She jerked her head in the direction of their son, who seemed to be giggling and having a whale of a time, despite the fact that he didn't speak more than a word or two of Kharastani. 'You think he looks deprived?'

'Not at the moment, no—but he will, Lex.'

'Oh, really?'

'Yes, really! He will become one of those fatherless boys who hang around on street corners and smoke cigarettes,' he said witheringly.

'Oh, ye of little faith! Where did you get your knowledge of the world from, Gio? The international book of stereotypes? And anyway—' She fixed him with a triumphant look '—You grew up without a father yourself!'

His smile told her that she had walked straight into the trap he had carefully set up for her. 'Exactly!' he breathed. 'And I have seen what it's like!'

Alexa frowned, confused now. 'You're saying that you don't like the way *you've* turned out?'

'I am saying that I have turned out the man I am *in spite of* my upbringing—but Paolo may not be so fortunate. I have seen what it is to have a mother who hungers for the company of men.'

'I've had *two* lovers in my life!' she returned furiously. 'And I've told you that until I'm blue in the face— when are you going to get it through your head, and believe that I'm not about to start entertaining the troops in my bedroom?'

'But you are still very young,' he parried. 'Your life is taken up with the mechanics of everyday life with Paolo. Yet there will come a time when he does not need you quite so much—and you will think about fulfilling your own sexual needs. That is when he is likely to go off the rails.'

'You didn't,' she pointed out. 'And you were the child of a single mother!'

'Because I was lucky!' he stormed, feeling a knife twist deep in his heart as he remembered all those nights waiting for his mother to come home. Not being able to settle until he heard the sound of her high heels as they clattered their way across the hall floor. Sometimes he would fall asleep, only waking with a start as he heard the front door being pulled to a close and realised that it was past dawn… 'But it's a lottery we're talking about,' he added. 'And Paolo might not be as lucky as I was.'

'*All* life is a lottery,' she said dryly, wondering if she had imagined that sudden bleakness which had clouded his eyes. She must have done—for now his face had resumed that flinty and obdurate expression. 'Having two parents isn't a surefire recipe for happiness, Gio.'

'No, but I want to maximise his chances,' he said stubbornly.

She shook her head in frustration, the bright sunlight making her squint. She wished that she could just grab her son and run. 'Were you always such a pessimist?'

'Pretty much,' he said softly. 'You base your behaviour on personal experience.'

She looked at him, trying to be objective—but it wasn't easy. His attitude riled her, and his words infuriated her, but that didn't stop her wanting to tangle her fingers in his thick black hair and pull his head down to kiss her. She swallowed. 'Look, you've given me plenty to think about, and I will,' she conceded. 'When I get back to England.'

Giovanni gave a grim kind of smile. She still hadn't realised, had she? That when he wanted something he went all out until he had got it.

'I don't think you understand,' he said silkily. 'The decision has already been taken.'

Alexa blinked, scarcely aware that in the distance could be heard the sound of pipes and drums, and that haunting, reedy instrument again. 'What decision?' she breathed, as the musicians began warming up.

'Things have moved on. I now accept that you are not a woman of loose morals, but you are still a woman, with all a woman's needs—and I am not prepared to tolerate my son being brought up by another man,' he said flatly.

'But this is all hypothetical, Giovanni,' she objected. 'There *isn't* another man.'

'Not at the moment, there isn't.'

Being told you couldn't have something often had the effect of making you want it more, and it provoked in Alexa a sudden defiance. 'You can't make me do anything I don't want to,' she said.

'Oh, but I can, *cara*,' he demurred softly. 'And I want Paolo with me.'

'Paolo lives with *me*,' she pointed out, aware that they were discussing their son as if he was a piece of furniture. Her cheeks began to burn with shame and terror.

'Then it is obvious that you must come and live with me as well,' he said silkily. 'You are a good mother, and I want the chance to be a good father. We proved last night that we've never stopped desiring one another— so where's the stumbling block?'

She wanted to blurt out and ask him what about *love*? Or even—if that was aiming too high—what about the emotional security she had discussed with his father? But his father had been as dismissive about it as Giovanni inevitably would. It would be as useless as chasing after rainbows—their colours always appeared so bright and solid from a distance—but when you got up close they were nothing but air.

Maybe what she and Giovanni had briefly shared all those years ago *had* been love—or the tentative beginnings of love—but it had been smashed by circumstance. Yet her heart still burned for him as much as her body did, and he was the father of her child. They were tied together through both their lifetimes by shared flesh and blood.

What he was offering was a compromise—but how would she have the strength to live a lifetime of compromise with the only man she had ever loved?

Alexa shook her head. 'I'm sorry, Giovanni, but I can't do it.'

There was silence for a moment, and when he spoke his words had all the deadly cutting power of a razor's edge.

'It isn't a proposal I'm making,' he said. 'It's a statement of fact.'

Alexa blinked. 'I don't understand.'

'Then you are being remarkably slow, if I might say so. I am not *asking* you to come and live with me, Lex— I am telling you that you have no alternative if you wish to remain with your son.'

Did he imagine that by coming to a country like Kharastan—where men dominated and women obeyed—he could simply dictate his terms and she would meekly accept them?

'There is *always* an alternative, Giovanni,' she said proudly.

His smile was one of cold, pure power.

'Yes, you are right,' he agreed softly, and for a moment saw her relax. 'You can hire yourself a lawyer to fight me—if you can afford to. But no matter how much money you were to pour into it, it would be to no avail, Lex. You see, if you do not accept my terms then there will be a custody battle—that I do not want but which will go ahead if it comes to it.'

His black eyes glittered with a determination which made her skin turn to ice. 'And I will win.'

CHAPTER TEN

GIOVANNI'S silken threat rather spoiled the rest of the day for Alexa. It wouldn't have mattered what had happened during the marriage celebrations—a rocket could have flown down from the moon in the middle of the ceremony itself, for all the notice Alexa would have taken. She guessed that there were worse places to worry that you were going to lose custody of your only child, but right then she couldn't think of one.

She forced herself to try and concentrate, so that the memory of such a magnificent day wouldn't be just a blur—and so that the royal family wouldn't consider her a churlish and ungrateful guest, or Paolo be ashamed of his Mamma for looking glum. And concentrating on the occasion worked well as a distraction technique.

The service took place in a circular courtyard in one of the most innermost sanctums of the palace, with tiered seating all around—especially constructed, according to Sorrel to accommodate all the visiting dignitaries. Alexa recognised two members of the British royal family, as well as three ex-presidents, and it was the strangest sensation to be sitting close enough to touch people she had previously only seen within the pages of a newspaper or on television.

Because, of course, given the Giovanni connection, they were sitting in the very best seats, listening to vows made in Kharastani, French and English, repeated in all three languages. She sat there with a fixed smile as thousands of fresh rose petals fluttered down from the balcony and there was a burst of applause and triumphant music.

Somehow she managed not to flinch at the blinding wall of flash from the cameras which exploded into life as Laura was officially made a princess. Afterwards, the wedding party walked on brilliant blue carpets, beneath garlands of jasmine and deep-scented lilies, to the feast itself—where every conceivable Kharastani delicacy was being served on priceless gold dishes inlaid with real jewels.

Alexa found herself wondering if any of the guests would be tempted to pocket one of the teaspoons, which looked as if they'd each be worth a small fortune—and the inappropriate thought made her smile properly for almost the first time.

'You're very quiet, *cara*,' observed Giovanni, as they walked towards the table.

'What did you expect?' she demanded in a low voice. 'That I'd be dancing with joy after the threats you made earlier?'

'I believe there *is* dancing later,' he observed evenly. 'So why not?'

'Oh, very clever. Well, count me out!'

Of course heartfelt declarations made to your estranged husband when you were having a row didn't always stand up to gentle pressure from well-meaning members of your brand-new 'family'. Thus, when the Sheikh made it known after the meal that he would like to have a photograph of himself with his two sons, their wives and Paolo, how could Alexa have possibly objected?

Then he called 'my most loyal and trusted aide' Malik' into the shot—though the reason for *that* was a little confusing. And when the entire wedding party had adjourned into the grand ballroom—which was bedecked with flowers—the Sheikh raised his hand to order the dancing to begin.

It was started by the bride and groom, and soon Zahir waved Alexa and Giovanni onto the dance floor—though she held herself as stiffly as a frozen piece of wood in his arms.

'It won't work, you know,' Giovanni said softly.

'What won't? I don't know what you're talking about.'

'Yes, you do. I'm talking about sulking, my *bella* Lex. It won't change my mind, and it will only make things unpleasant for Paolo—and ultimately for you.'

Alexa raised her eyebrows. 'So not only am I being blackmailed into remaining as your wife—I'm also being instructed on how to behave?'

'That all depends.'

'On?'

'How good you're going to be.'

'I don't *feel* like being good!'

'Ah!' He started laughing. 'That's better,' he murmured approvingly. Giovanni's hand moved down to the small of her back and began to massage its knotted tension with expert caress. 'Don't fight it, *cara*.'

He meant *Don't fight me*. And, oh, it was so tempting to obey him. To sink into his embrace and let the hard heat of his body send little sizzles all the way down her nerve endings. Especially when the rhythmic movement of his fingers was easing all the rigidity out of her body, making it feel as squishy as marshmallow.

Alexa closed her eyes and ran her tongue over dry lips with something approaching despair. What was it about Giovanni, and only Giovanni, that he could make her feel this way? She hadn't lived *completely* as a hermit during her time as a single mother. There had been the occasional social function—some of them with dancing, and some of them even with eligible men had who seemed keen to dance with her. But it had never felt like this.

'How long is it since we've danced?' he questioned unsteadily.

'I…don't remember.'

'Don't you? It was the night of our own wedding.'

Of course she remembered—she had just been trying not to. Though she was surprised that *he* did. Her head seemed to want to fall into the hollow of his shoulder, just as it had done back then. She could feel the slow build-up of sexual hunger. Much more of this and she would be incapacitated by it. Alexa wriggled, but the movement brought her body into frighteningly erotic proximity to the ridge of hardness she could feel quite clearly through the fine silk of his robes. Her eyes widened into saucers. 'Giovanni!'

'Can you feel what you do to me?' he questioned idly.

'Stop it!'

'How? There's only one way to get rid of it, and I don't think it's going to happen right now—in the circumstances.'

'You're disgusting!'

'You didn't seem to think so last night!'

'That was different.'

'*How* was it different, Lex?'

'Well, for a start I didn't realise then that you were planning to fight me for custody of Paolo!'

'You thought that after the wedding we'd all go back to our separate lives—as if nothing had happened?'

'No, of course not.'

'What, then?'

The music changed tempo and mercifully picked up speed, so that Alexa could move her body marginally away from the aroused distraction of his. 'I thought we'd do what other couples in similar circumstances do. We'd make access arrangements.'

'*Access* arrangements? You want to fly a young child out to Italy on alternate weekends.'

'Or…well, there's always holidays.' As soon as she saw the darkening fury on his face she knew that she had said the wrong thing.

'A part-time father, you mean?' he snapped. 'Still, I suppose that's an improvement on an absentee father.'

'That's not what I'm suggesting. I'm just not sure how Paolo would feel about being uprooted to Italy.'

As usual, she was tagging her own misgivings onto Paolo, he thought. 'Why don't you ask him? Or don't you dare to hear the answer he may give you?'

'Oh, Gio.' She looked up at him with wide eyes. 'It's not like that at all.'

'Isn't it?' He pulled her back into his arms—only this time she was aware of his strength, rather than his sexuality as he bent his head to look directly into her beautiful face. Did she think for a second that all she had to do was to bat those amazing pale green eyes at him and he would accede to whatever she wanted? 'I don't think you appreciate how *lenient* I'm being with you—considering that I have been kept on the sidelines for all these years,' he hissed. 'Maybe it's about time I laid down a few ground rules.' His black eyes glittered with pure rage. 'You will co-operate with me, and you will do so at once.'

'At *once*?'

'On your return to England, you will make the necessary arrangements.'

'*Arrangements*?' she echoed again, sounding like one of those language tapes where you repeated the words so that you would never forget them.

'For your move to Naples,' he finished, with a gritty kind of smile.

Her knees felt suddenly weak as she recognised that he meant every word. He wasn't going to back off now, or have some miraculous change of heart—and even if he did would access ever really work? What if Paolo became enraptured of his macho daddy, seduced by his power and his money? Wouldn't a tiny rented cottage with underwear drying in the bathroom begin to pale as he became old enough to make comparisons—as label-conscious teenagers inevitably did?

Afraid that she might do something unforgivable—like cry at a wedding when the slushy part was over—Alexa pulled away from him. 'I think I've had enough dancing for now. It's late. I'm…I'm going to find Paolo and put him to bed.'

He traced a thoughtful finger around the outline of her lips. 'You can run from me all you like, but it will be to no avail,' he said softly. 'Because soon you will be with me in Naples—exactly where I want you to be, Lex. Just as later you will be in my arms and in my bed.'

Alexa felt her mouth tremble beneath his touch, even though her heart rebelled. Did he think that because he was the son of the Sheikh that he could imperiously impose his desire upon her?

'No, I won't,' she vowed, and went to move away. But he stayed her with a hand to her arm, his hard fingers biting into the soft silk of her skin.

'And while we're at it let's get something else straight—which is that I'm not prepared to play cat-and-mouse with you over sex,' he hissed. 'Especially when we've established just how much you want it. Last night was an exception—but I have neither the time nor the inclination to go through that kind of pantomime night after night.'

'You ripping off my nightie, you mean?' she accused.

Giovanni froze. 'It pleases you to make it sound like an aggressive act, doesn't it, Lex—even when such things are done within the bedroom and only serve to heighten sexual pleasure?' Like it did yours, he thought bitterly—and then wondered if she would be too much of a hypocrite to admit it.

'Well, I don't want you near me tonight,' she said, terrified that her voice would crack, and that tears would start spilling out of the corners of her eyes to show him that beneath it all she was just a vulnerable and pathetic walkover. 'So stay away.'

Giovanni's face hardened in a proud and arrogant look. Did she really believe that he would beg her? Or weaken when she called his bluff? He bent his head close to her face, so that all she could see was the ebony blaze of his eyes. 'If I don't find you in our bed tonight, I shall not come to you. You can attempt to withhold sex as a bargaining tool, but it won't work—for believe me when I tell you that I shall not change my mind about Paolo.'

He walked off the dance floor, with every female eye following him, and Alexa was shaking as she went over to lead the over-excited and exhausted Paolo to bed. After she had tucked him up, she ran herself a bath and lay there in the cooling water, telling herself over and over again that she would *not* be intimidated and that there was no way she was going to be an easy conquest. Not any more.

How much loveless sex could she endure before she blurted out something unforgivable? Like telling him that she wanted the kind of intimacy she had once thought was hers for the taking because he had loved her enough to marry her? Would Giovanni meet her halfway if she dared try? Or was he too hard and unforgiving to ever be able to let go of the past?

Her skin was pink and her fingertips as wrinkled as starfish by the time she emerged from the bathroom in her nightgown.

The salon was empty, and in the bedroom the vast bed lay uninhabited—mocking her with its bareness. Alexa knew that she just *couldn't* go in there and wait for him like a sacrificial lamb. Instead, she crept silently towards the divan, where last night he had begun his seduction, and there she lay, waiting for what seemed like hours as her heart skittered with apprehension. When he came should she suggest that they talk—properly—and try to do so without blame or recrimination?

As the minutes ticked by, her nervousness began to seep away slowly replaced by the drugging onslaught of sleep. And Alexa welcomed it—embraced it, almost—for at least sleep would rob her of these tortured thoughts and the aching sense of realisation that the control over her own life seemed to be slipping away from her. Could Gio *really* force her and Paolo to stay with him in Naples? was her last conscious memory.

Giovanni walked towards the silent suite, rubbing his fingers against tired temples. After meeting with various Italian dignitaries, his father had summoned him to his private quarters and offered him land on the eastern reaches of the country—and a permanent home if he so desired. But inheritance had been the last thing on Giovanni's mind. He had been more stirred by the impact of sharing time with this man who did not have time on his side.

They had talked long into the night, until the Sheikh had grown tired and there had been only one thought dominating all others in Giovanni's mind.

That Paolo should never experience the absence of a father figure as he had done.

'Do you blame me for not having acknowledged you sooner?' the Sheikh had asked him quietly.

Giovanni had given his father a rueful smile. 'It is not my duty to apportion blame—only to learn from the experience.' He had agreed that he would return soon to Kharastan and to discuss the future then. He yawned. A wedding, a true reconciliation and the proud presentation of his only son to his brand-new family. Yes, it had been one hell of a day—and it was not over yet. Symbolically, Giovanni knew that one final test lay ahead, and he felt the sudden anticipatory hammer of his heart.

Did Alexa wish to be his wife in the fullest sense of the word?

The corridors to their suite were almost deserted, and when he walked through the dimly lit rooms he found her lying curled up on the divan, swathed in bedlinen. He felt the knife-twist of anger and frustration deep in his gut, and a sudden weariness, too. Oh, foolish woman! Did she not realise that he had made a vow, and that his arrogant Neapolitan pride would never allow him to go back on it?

Did she not realise that up until now he had been handling her with kidgloves?

And that now she stood to lose everything?

CHAPTER ELEVEN

THOSE last few days in Kharastan taught Alexa the true meaning of isolation—and she was quickly made aware that her refusal to share Giovanni's bed had effected a kind of stand-off between them. Something was different, and it was her husband's attitude towards her. Gone was the gleam of desire, and the teasingly provocative remarks, and Alexa realised the truth in the saying that indifference was death.

His demeanour was haughty and icy towards her. If he was sexually frustrated then he was too proud to show it—and much too proud to ask her to change her mind, or to try and change it for her. She was left in no doubt of how it felt to be an outsider.

In a world full of privilege—to be royal was always to be top of the heap, no matter which society you were in, and in that Kharastan was no different from any other.

Giovanni was the favoured son. The Sheikh's son. Yes, she was afforded courtesy and respect because she was his wife, but more importantly because she was Paolo's mother. Yet deep down she knew that if

Giovanni chose to withdraw his support then she would be cast aside. Cut socially adrift and left to flounder.

No one was actually *rude* to her, but she sensed a certain coolness and a sense of detachment—almost as if they considered it a waste of time to include her in any important discussions about the future, because she would not be part of that future.

Alexa began to question whether she had been too hasty. Whether she *was* using sex as some kind of weapon. And so much of sex was in the head, wasn't it? At least that was what they said, especially about women. By deliberately sleeping on the divan on the night of the wedding itself, she seemed to have wounded Giovanni's macho male pride in a way she hadn't really appreciated. His eyes had glimmered at her coldly the following morning, and Alexa had been left feeling strangely empty and confused—questioning whether she'd done the right thing.

After that, he remained exaggeratedly cool towards her as they made all the preparations for her trip to Naples, and she supposed that his demeanour was perfectly understandable in the circumstances. So why did it niggle away at her? Wasn't this what she'd wanted? To show him that she would not be bought, like some kind of modern-day concubine?

But it went much deeper than just the act of sex itself. Of course the sex worked—it always had done—and she suspected there wasn't a woman on the planet who wouldn't be turned on and satisfied by Giovanni. It was what the sex *stood* for that scared her. Functional, emotionless sex was scary—it felt insubstantial. After it was over it left her feeling *less than*—as if she would disappear if she wasn't careful—and maybe that was what he really wanted.

But, nonetheless, she caved in to his wishes to go to Italy—because she didn't have the strength or the resources to do otherwise. Arrangements had already been made for Paolo to transfer to a small bi-lingual school in Naples, which had lemon trees growing all around it and a white rabbit called Blanco, which the children took in turns to pet and which her son had fallen in love during their visit. And *that* was the main reason she intended to give Naples a chance. She tried to put it into words to Teri, during their brief return to England to tie up all the loose ends.

'My happiness is all linked with Paolo's,' she admitted tentatively. 'It's not something separate from him. And he *wants* the change, Teri—he wants it badly. He loves his…Papà…which is exactly as it should be.' She said the words with determination, as she knew they should be said—though wasn't there a tiny, horrible part of her which wanted Paolo to declare that he never wished to see Giovanni again? It would certainly make life easier.

'And he loves Italy, too,' she continued. 'Who wouldn't—especially when you're his age? Everyone makes a fuss of him out there, and not just because he's Giovanni's son—they genuinely seem to love children. They pinch his cheeks and try to give him sweets. Then there's the weather, of course—and the swimming pool. It's going to be like a permanent holiday for him.'

No, the decision had been made. They were going to Naples—and no amount of avoiding sex with Giovanni in Kharastan was going to change his mind. He had made that quite clear. Thus the court case and custody battle would now be avoided.

Paolo was excited—desperately—and Alexa knew she should not minimise the impact of such a gigantic lifestyle-change on her son. At the moment he saw only the rich and exciting aspects of the move, but doubtless he would miss his homeland, and all his little friends. She had to make the transition easy for him, and bury whatever *she* was feeling deep inside her.

But when they arrived in Naples and Giovanni drove them through the winding streets—past cafés, cathedrals and archaeological excavations—Alexa began to relax a little, remembering the bustling and colourful impression that the city had made on her when she'd arrived as an impressionable twenty-something.

Paolo was gazing wide-eyed out of the car window, but Alexa found that she kept wanting to snatch a look at the hard, chiselled lines of Giovanni's dark profile.

'It doesn't look as if it's changed much,' she observed, trying to concentrate on the lively chaos outside and not his cool manner towards her.

Giovanni shot her a glance as he hit the flat of his hand on the horn, in typically Neapolitan fashion. 'Look beneath the surface and you'll find that everything changes,' he said obliquely, as the car began to climb the hill which led out of the crowded city centre towards Vomero, and the family home. 'A lot of money has been poured into the city. The poorer areas are being regenerated—a huge clean-up campaign has been instigated. Napoli has had a face-lift—and she wants the world to see it.'

'Are we nearly there, Papà?' piped up Paolo.

Giovanni smiled. '*Si, mio bello.* Nearly here,' he said, glancing down at his son, his heart turning over with love—and then he caught sight of Alexa's pale face in the driving mirror, and his hands tensed on the wheel. 'Remember this?' he questioned harshly, as a tall pair of electronic gates opened to reveal the elegant façade of the *palazzo* beyond.

Alexa had only visited the place once, years ago— the cool, dark villa where he'd grown up, which nestled in the hill as if it had always been there. 'Yes,' she answered uncertainly.

Giovanni felt a shiver momentarily chilling his skin. The house had been empty since his mother's death, and just the smell and feel of it now made him apprehensive as the ghosts of his past floated before him.

But his waterside apartment was not suitable for the three of them, and this was one of the best locations in which to bring up a family. So he had hired a cook, and a housekeeper who had a son, Fabrizio, who was just a year older than Paolo. At least there would be plenty to keep his son amused, he thought. He could learn football, and Italian, and some warm southern sun would bring the colour to his pale English cheeks.

'He can start school as soon as he likes,' Giovanni said, during dinner that first evening.

And what about me? her eyes asked him silently, her fingers crumbling an unwanted piece of bread.

'You can decorate the house and improve your Italian,' Giovanni said carelessly. 'Or shop.'

He made her sound as dispensable as yesterday's newspaper—which presumably had been his intention.

The meal was being served outside on the terrace, which looked down the hillside. Stars like bright lamps hung suspended from the night sky, and Naples glittered like a jewelled brooch in the distance.

Alexa kept looking down to the city, thinking, *This is my home now.* She wondered if it would ever feel that way—but the thought of the future scared her. What if it stayed like this—with her and Giovanni skirting round each other like strangers who had just met at a cocktail party?

But that was precisely the pattern of the days to come—with Alexa feeling like the water which had been pushed out to the edge of a whirlpool, while Paolo was sucked further and further into the centre of his father's life.

To see her son blossom beneath the sun and the approving eye of his father was both sweet and poignant, and Alexa began to understand that a moral obligation could be far stronger than a legal threat. Because she wasn't stupid.

Now that she had stepped back from their heated exchanges she realised that there was no way Giovanni could *force* them to stay—and that no court would wrench her son away from her simply because his father was rich and powerful.

But how could she wrench Paolo away—when he was clearly so happy here—take him back to a life which would always seem like a half-life in comparison?

At night she lay in the cool, scented room she had been given, listening to the massed sound of the cicadas whirring outside her window—but really listening out for Giovanni. Wondering if she would ever hear the creak of his footstep outside, or the sound of her door slowly opening—and then cursing herself for her own foolishness.

Did she really picture him walking into her room and climbing silently into bed beside her? When he'd already warned her that if she rejected him a second time he would withdraw from her? When he was a combination of two proud and stubborn races—probably the least likely candidate in the world to backtrack?

Or had she somehow thought that his was an idle threat, and that he'd change his mind and stroke her hair and tell her it was all going to be okay? Hadn't she realised that the ice she had been skating on was so thin that it was almost transparent?

Night after night she would turn over, pulling the fine sweet-scented Egyptian cotton sheet over her narrow shoulders and asking herself, couldn't *she* go to *him*?

But the longer Alexa gave the matter consideration, the more daunting a prospect it seemed. To have to creep into the bed of a man who had only offered you sex as part of an irresistible package to gain his son wouldn't fill even the most confident woman with much in the way of self-esteem. Wasn't that settling for crumbs when she wanted the meat of a real relationship, with love and closeness and all the other stuff which went with it?

But Giovanni didn't *do* love. He did jealousy, suspicion and distance. When he was having sex he held something back—hell, he *always* held something back, whatever he did. Would some women be content with that? Would *she*?

She stared up at the ceiling. It was funny how you could tell yourself you wanted x, y and z out of a relationship—but in the end you were defeated by the ache in your body and the emptiness in your heart.

CHAPTER TWELVE

'MAMMA, did you *know* that Naples football pitch is called Stadio San *Paolo*?'

Alexa smiled. 'No, darling, I didn't.'

'Is that why you called me Paolo?' her son demanded.

Alexa's fingers trembled slightly as she put her coffee cup down in the saucer and met Giovanni's enigmatic black eyes. 'N-no. I called you Paolo because it's a lovely name.'

Giovanni heaped some *marmellata di albicocche* onto his bread . 'I thought I'd take Paolo down to the stadium this morning—Fabrizio, too. Then maybe have some pizza down by the waterside.' He paused. 'You want to come?'

She could see the effort it took for him to ask her, and knew the effort it would take her to maintain a façade of contentment for a whole day down in the city. Sometimes she could carry it off almost without thinking, but others— like today—it felt like a weighty burden which was chained to her shoulders with no chance of shaking it off.

Alexa shook her head. 'No, thanks. I thought I'd

carry on going through the swatches of fabric for the library curtains—and I've found a book on fifteenth Century wall colours.'

Giovanni shrugged as he finished his breakfast and put his napkin on the table. Naturally she would prefer to sit alone in a dusty library than to spend any time with *him*. 'As you wish,' he said coolly, and stood up. 'We'll be back around five.'

'In time for a swim, Papà?'

'*Si, bambino.*' Giovanni's eyes crinkled automatically. 'In time for a swim.'

But Giovanni's heart was heavy as the two of them went off to find Fabrizio—the golden promise of the day ahead tainted with the certain knowledge that he could not go on like this. He stared up at the cloudless blue sky. None of them could. It was not fair—but especially to Alexa. He had seen the sadness behind her smile—a sadness she did her best to conceal, but in a way that only made it glaringly more apparent. Unexpectedly, her silent suffering hurt. Made him feel a tyrant—like some throwback to another time, when powerful men could get their own way by sheer force of will and power.

Had he really imagined that they could carry on like this—into an unknown future—with Alexa here only on sufferance?

Yes, he wanted his son full-time—but that was never going to be the case. Not when he had blackmailed his mother and coerced her into staying. No wonder she recoiled from him whenever he walked into the room.

If it had been any other woman than Alexa he might

have tried to seduce her into staying—but that was not an option. And not simply because as a measure to keep her here it would be only temporary. No, it was because he had grown to respect her—to admire her quiet dignity and the way she conducted herself around him and around their son.

She deserved that respect, but she deserved something else too—and that was her freedom.

Giovanni's eyes narrowed against the sun as a cloud passed over his heart.

After they'd gone, Alexa set to work. She suspected that Giovanni had been being flippant when he'd first suggested she decorate the villa, but she had seized the task with vigour—partly as a kind of displacement activity, but also knowing she would never get an opportunity like this again.

The *palazzo* was old, with dim, muted rooms abounding with superb eighteenth-century art, multi-coloured marble and Majolica tiles which were worth a small fortune. There was a formal *salone*, the dining room, and a more informal room which overlooked the garden, where tall cypress trees rose like stately dark green flames. But it was the library which had captivated her, with its row upon row of leather-bound books—all with their own delicious scent and texture. It was the kind of place she could get lost in—allowing her imagination to run riot among the well-loved novels in different languages and the reference books—some with rich and wonderful illustrations.

The decor had been badly neglected, and was crying out for some tender loving care. Alexa had managed to find an oil-based paint which exactly matched the original tempera which had adorned the walls. Later, she would show it to Giovanni, to see if it met with his approval.

And will you be around to see it painted? mocked a small voice in her head. But she shushed it quiet and sat back on her heels to drink in the room's beauty, and at that moment a shelf which was almost hidden by the fireplace caught her attention.

She could see the corner of a book sticking out, and closer investigation revealed it to be a photo album. As she pulled it out Alexa stilled, with shock because… Well, because it was a pictorial record of Giovanni's childhood.

And it was like staring down at her own son.

Wasn't it funny how she could know something on one level—that Paolo's resemblance to his father was uncanny—but seeing it captured on the page for the first time took her breath away?

There was Giovanni at a circus, standing in a sweet little coat next to an elephant. Were elephants safe? Alexa wondered inconsequentially, as she turned the page.

There was Giovanni smiling next to his mother, by the seaside down in Chiaia, and there they were in Paris, walking among the flowers in the Tuilleries. There was a record of Gio in just about every country in Europe, and every photo was distinguished by his mother gazing into the eyes of a tall and handsome man.

And it was a different man in every photo.

She looked closely at the image of the child who so

resembled Paolo and saw the confusion and vulnerability in his young face. This wasn't a boy enjoying
a rip-roaring series of holidays—this was a boy who was
an appendage, an extra. A boy who funded a rich and
expensive lifestyle. A little boy lost.

Oh, Gio, she thought.

'What the hell do you think you're doing?'

The words broke into her thoughts, and with a start
Alexa looked up to see Giovanni framed in the doorway
of the library, an implacable look darkening his face, the
whole stance of his body tense and watchful as his black
gaze swept over her.

She sat back on her heels again, her heart beating
very fast. 'Looking around.'

'*Impicciona*!' he accused.

The word shot out like a bullet—an obscure word,
but wasn't the human memory a strange and selective
thing? For its meaning came back to her as if she used
it every day of the week. Alexa shook her head. 'No, I'm
not snooping.'

His glance swept over to the window—to the
panorama of the verdant countryside, culminating in that
heart-stopping aspect of Naples which was so beautiful
that you could understand where the expression *See
Naples and die* came from. Some views were almost
priceless, such was their beauty—and this was one of
them. A stunning vista bought by a sheikh in order to
guarantee his mother's silence. Buying a woman's com-
pliance was not a trait he admired in his father—and yet
wasn't he guilty of attempting to do the same with Alexa?

This morning, when he had gone with his son down to the city and felt the grip of the child's trusting hand in his, he had felt his heart breaking open with happiness. Only to be left with a sickly scar of realisation in its wake.

It had hit him like another thunderbolt—that what he desired above all else was love. And love could not be bought, nor forced, nor demanded. Love was like a plant—it needed nurturing and light and space in order to thrive. All the things he had denied Alexa when they'd first been married, because of his stupid, arrogant pride.

He wanted the kind of authentic, warm family life that he had never had for himself—but he couldn't have that without the mother of his only child there. And Alexa didn't want to be there. Being there, with him, in Naples, was the *last* thing she wanted—she had told him that herself—and could he blame her? For he had tried to keep her there as an emotional prisoner—tied to him by false threats of how he would ruin her if she failed to comply with his unreasonable demands.

He had been angered by her failure to tell him about his son—but in view of his behaviour both before and since the discovery could he really blame her? How could he possibly berate her for her deception when she must have known that once he found out he would move heaven and earth in an attempt to possess Paolo in the way he had once tried to possess her?

For all the mess they had made of their own relationship, no one—least of all him—was denying that she was a good mother. So was *this* how he was attempting to reward her for her exemplary care of his son? By intimidating her?

He would tell her now that he would be generous with her. 'You can have the alimony you deserve. Enough to guarantee you a life of comfort in England. I won't try to keep you here against your will any longer, Lex.' He shrugged. 'You can go.'

Alexa blinked, taken aback. '*Go?*'

Did she wish to twist the knife? To make him beg for her forgiveness? 'Yes—go!' he said angrily. 'For that is what you wish!'

The freedom and the financial security he was offering her beckoned, and Alexa suddenly realised that these things meant nothing. But then she was beginning to understand what motivated this powerful but ultimately lonely man.

Alexa stared into his face for a long moment. His jealousy had started the chain of events which had led to her keeping their child a secret—but she had never stopped to question *why* it was etched so sharply on his character. It was almost as if she had imagined he'd been born with it—in the same way that he'd been born with black eyes and olive skin.

But people didn't just inherit jealousy—it wasn't up there with eye colour and long, lean legs. It developed for a reason—and the reason was there in black and white, and in colour, too—locked within the pages of his childhood photograph album.

A different man on every page—with Giovanni's discomfiture plain to see. Alexa knew that little boys were notoriously protective of their mothers, and that children often over-simplified life, based on their own experience of it. Paolo had taken to Gio perhaps because he'd felt some primitive bond straight away, but his acceptance had almost certainly been helped by the fact that he was the first man—the only man—she'd been intimate with since his conception.

She tried to imagine Paolo's confusion and rage if she had brought in a succession of 'uncles' to part-share his life. Was it any wonder that Giovanni had grown up thinking that women liked variety rather than constancy?

That was why he had overreacted on their wedding night she realised. Not because she wasn't innocent—but because of what her lack of virginity stood for. Virginity implied inexperience. Virginity was *safe*—from it he would know as much of her back-story as he needed to. He had thought her a goddess and discovered that she was just a woman. And the role-model he'd been exposed to as a child had made him uneasy.

Emotionally, he had flailed out at her like a little boy, and her *perceived* deception about her virginity had then been compounded by her *real* deception over their child. Both of them had acted rashly and selfishly—but as she stared into his eyes Alexa realised that she couldn't keep hiding behind her fear and the mistakes of the past for ever. Someone had to cross this ever-widening chasm, and if she had to embrace humility to do so—well, there were a lot worse things than that.

'I'm sorry, Giovanni,' she whispered. 'So…very sorry.'

He had been mentally assessing how best to work at

formalising their separation, and her words came as a
shock. He froze, his black eyes narrowing into ebony
shards. 'Is there something you've done that I should
know about?'

'No. It's nothing like that.' She hesitated. 'I meant for
the pain I've caused you. For the years of Paolo's life
I've denied you.'

He shook his head, angry now. He wanted her to
leave well alone—to leave him to come to terms with
his decision. 'You don't have to say these things, Alexa.
You can have your freedom. You can go home to
England as soon as you wish.'

Was he sending her away in any case? Alexa stared
at him aghast. 'And what if…?' Flicking the tip of her
tongue around her lips, she swallowed. 'What if I don't
want to go home to England?'

'Don't,' he said flatly. For the steel barriers around
his heart had been in place for too long to be vanquished
by a stumbled denial, however prettily she made it.
'Don't say things you don't mean.'

'But I *do* mean it! I…' She hesitated, knowing that
she had to put her feelings on the line, and knowing also
that there was no guarantee he would treat them with
anything other than mistrust or contempt. This was the
hardest thing to say when the face you were saying
them to looked like a stony mask. 'I love you, Giovanni,'
she whispered. 'Deep down I've never stopped loving
you, and I never will.'

The words shot through him like little darts.
Deliberately, he turned his back on her, blocking out the

look of naked appeal in her eyes and concealing the hunger in his own eyes, too—such a raw and savage hunger. Not for her body, nor even for their son—but for the dream which had eluded him all his life.

He wanted to turn back to her, to tell her that *he* was sorry too, for the twists and turns their lives had taken, but he was scared—strong, powerful and autocratic Giovanni da Verrazzano was actually *scared*. What if these things were simply being said carelessly—here today and forgotten tomorrow?

Yet as he turned and looked into her face he found himself believing her. The truth blazed out like a beacon from those shining green eyes. Maybe it had been there all along—he just hadn't known how to look for it. He had something wonderful within his grasp, but everything to lose—and he didn't think he could bear to lose it. Not for a second time.

'I don't want your words,' he said harshly. For how could words undo all the bitterness of the past, all the wounds they had knowingly and unknowingly inflicted on each other?

'Then take my heart,' she said softly, walking up to him, touching her fingertips to his tense face. 'Take everything I have. But please, Giovanni—take me with you on your journey through life. I don't care if you don't love me back—just so long as you stay a good father to our son. And I will stay faithful to you, my one true love— as I have done since the first time you took me into your arms. And, besides, I have enough love to go round.'

There was a pause. He felt the slam of his heart and

the kick of some powerful emotion deep inside him—
as if some great block of ice had suddenly been melted
by the furnace within. For a moment he didn't move,
and then, when he did, so did she—and they clung to
each other like two survivors from a shipwreck.

A sigh shuddered from his lips and washed over her
mouth as they began to kiss, and it was a kiss like no
other they had shared. For it was not one of lust or anger
or frustration, it was a symbol of their love—real, adult
love—and it was their commitment to their future.
Because through the tears and the joy Alexa sensed that
they would never again be parted.

At first neither of them noticed that a small boy had
crept into the library, and when they did they saw the look
of tentative hope on his little face. Together, they opened
their arms to their son—and he went right into them.

EPILOGUE

SHEIKH ZAHIR was delighted but apparently not surprised that Alexa and Giovanni had quietly renewed their wedding vows in Naples—and he insisted on throwing an enormous party for them in Kharastan. Teri was invited, and naturally Alexa's mother—'*Darling! You've done better than I could ever have dreamed!*'—as well as some of Paolo's little school friends and his old childminder.

But during the six months since they had last seen him, the Sheikh had grown more frail. Alexa remarked on it to Giovanni when they were lying in their huge palace bedroom, with the faint smell of jasmine-scented breeze wafting over their naked bodies.

Giovanni stared at the ceiling. 'I know,' he said, in a sombre voice. 'I do not think that he has long left.'

Alexa was aware of the bond which had been forged between father and son, two proud men who had difficulty expressing emotions—one because the starchy formality of duty forbade it, and the other because he had never been shown how. But Giovanni was getting better at it every day. Oh, yes. She turned to him and stroked her finger softly over the hard contours of his lean face.

'Do you want to come and live out here, *caro*?' She asked Giovanni softly. 'You're older than Xavier. Do you think Zahir wants to pass the kingdom on to you? Has he said anything about it?'

He turned and smiled and kissed the tip of her nose, marvelling in this woman who was his wife in every sense of the word. This woman who cared not for the trappings of wealth, nor for status, nor trinkets—her heart's desire lay in those closest to her, and mirrored his. Her family. He shook his dark head. 'Don't worry about it,' he murmured.

'You can't just pass it off like that, Gio!' she protested. 'And I'm not worried about *it*—I'm worried about *you*! What if—'

'Shh,' he whispered, and silenced her with a kiss. 'Just wait.'

The following day a formal announcement was made—that the last of the Sheikh's three sons was to be identified.

'*Another* son?' demanded Alexa, as the excited buzz of chatter grew around the capital. 'You mean the Sheikh's got a *third* son?'

Giovanni nodded. 'The third and *final* son, I am assured,' he said dryly.

Alexa stared at Giovanni with wide eyes. 'You aren't surprised?'

Giovanni laughed. 'No, I'm not—for the hell of me I can't work out why, but I was kind of expecting it.

Xavier and I were informed just before the announcement was made.'

'And do you know who it is?'

'No—although I was given the opportunity to do so. But Xavier and I said we would prefer to find out at the same time as our wives.'

'Oh, *Gio*!' she gurgled delightedly.

'Anyway, I've guessed. It's Malik.'

'*Malik?*'

'I'd stake my fortune on it.'

But he didn't have to. Because he was right. The Sheikh's loyal and trusted aide—the only one with pure Kharastani blood running through his veins was—in fact, the oldest son and Zahir's true heir.

Alexa had grown fond of Malik, but her first and most fervent loyalty was to her beloved husband.

'Did you imagine that you might have ruled Kharastan before you found out about Malik? And would you have done it?'

'I would have had no choice,' Giovanni said simply. 'Destiny is not something which can be chosen at will— like goods in a supermarket—and if my destiny had been to take over the mantle from my father, then I would have embraced it wholeheartedly.'

She would have been a sheikha, thought Alexa fleetingly—and their son would, have one day worn the crown. Suddenly she was glad for Paolo—rejoicing that such a great burden would not be placed upon shoulders which had already carried much in their young life. 'You don't mind?' she asked her husband anxiously. 'That you won't be Sheikh and rule this beautiful land?'

Giovanni smiled as he lifted his hand to her face with an air of wonder of his own—but then, he still hadn't lost that *Am I going to wake up in a minute feeling?* she always induced in him. How had she so transformed his life? he wondered. But he knew the answer—love had a transformative power like no other. For both of them. He had seen Alexa blossom and bloom like a flower as she basked in the warmth of his love.

'No, *amata mia*, I do not mind—for I have riches far greater than those contained in any kingdom.' His black eyes crinkled with their now-familiar smile as he raised her fingertips to his lips in the regal gesture which came so naturally to him. 'I have you, and I have Paolo—what more could any man ask from his life than that?'

**From the magnificent Blue Palace to the wild
plains of the desert, be swept away as three
sheikh princes find their brides.**

When English girl Sorrel announces she wishes to
explore the pleasures of the West, Sheikh Malik
must take action—if she wants to learn the ways
of seduction, he will be the one to teach her....

THE DESERT KING'S
VIRGIN BRIDE

by Sharon Kendrick

Book #2628

Coming in May 2007.

BRIDES OF CONVENIENCE

Forced into marriage—
by a millionaire!

Read these four wedding stories
in this new collection by your
favorite authors, available in
Promotional Presents May 2007:

THE LAWYER'S CONTRACT MARRIAGE
by Amanda Browning

A CONVENIENT WIFE
by Sara Wood

THE ITALIAN'S VIRGIN BRIDE
by Trish Morey

THE MEDITERRANEAN HUSBAND
by Catherine Spencer

Available for the first time at retail outlets this May!

Wined, dined and swept away by a British billionaire!

Don't be late!

**He's suave and sophisticated.
He's undeniably charming.
And above all, he treats her like a lady.**

But don't be fooled....

**Beneath the tux, there's a primal passionate lover
who's determined to make her his!**

Gabriella is in love with wealthy Rufus Gresham,
but he believes she's a gold digger.
Then they are forced to marry.... Will Rufus use
this as an excuse to get Gabriella in his bed?

Another British billionaire is coming your way in May 2007.

WIFE BY CONTRACT, MISTRESS BY DEMAND
by Carole Mortimer

Book #2633

REQUEST YOUR FREE BOOKS!

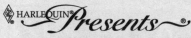

2 FREE NOVELS PLUS 2 FREE GIFTS!

YES! Please send me 2 FREE Harlequin Presents® novels and my 2 FREE gifts. After receiving them, if I don't wish to receive any more books, I can return the shipping statement marked "cancel." If I don't cancel, I will receive 6 brand-new novels every month and be billed just $3.80 per book in the U.S., or $4.47 per book in Canada, plus 25¢ shipping and handling per book and applicable taxes, if any*. That's a savings of close to 15% off the cover price! I understand that accepting the 2 free books and gifts places me under no obligation to buy anything. I can always return a shipment and cancel at any time. Even if I never buy another book from Harlequin, the two free books and gifts are mine to keep forever.

106 HDN EEXK 306 HDN EEXV

Name	(PLEASE PRINT)	
Address		Apt. #
City	State/Prov.	Zip/Postal Code

Signature (if under 18, a parent or guardian must sign)

Mail to the **Harlequin Reader Service**®:
IN U.S.A.: P.O. Box 1867, Buffalo, NY 14240-1867
IN CANADA: P.O. Box 609, Fort Erie, Ontario L2A 5X3

Not valid to current Harlequin Presents subscribers.

Want to try two free books from another line?
Call 1-800-873-8635 or visit www.morefreebooks.com.

* Terms and prices subject to change without notice. NY residents add applicable sales tax. Canadian residents will be charged applicable provincial taxes and GST. This offer is limited to one order per household. All orders subject to approval. Credit or debit balances in a customer's account(s) may be offset by any other outstanding balance owed by or to the customer. Please allow 4 to 6 weeks for delivery.

Your Privacy: Harlequin is committed to protecting your privacy. Our Privacy Policy is available online at www.eHarlequin.com or upon request from the Reader Service. From time to time we make our lists of customers available to reputable firms who may have a product or service of interest to you. If you would prefer we not share your name and address, please check here. ☐

HP07

Silhouette Desire

Introducing talented new author

TESSA RADLEY

*making her Silhouette Desire debut
this April with*

BLACK WIDOW BRIDE

Book #1794
Available in April 2007.

Wealthy Damon Asteriades had no choice but to
force Rebecca Grainger back to his family's estate—
despite his vow to keep away from her seductive
charms. But being so close to the woman society once
dubbed the Black Widow Bride had him aching to
claim her as his own...at any cost.

On sale April from Silhouette Desire!

Available wherever books are sold,
including most bookstores, supermarkets,
discount stores and drugstores.

Men who can't be tamed...or so they think!

Damien Wynter is as handsome and arrogant as sin.
He will lead jilted Sydney heiress Charlotte to the altar and
then make her pregnant—and to hell with the scandal!

If you love *Ruthless* men, look out for

THE BILLIONAIRE'S
SCANDALOUS MARRIAGE

by Emma Darcy

Book #2627

Coming in May 2007.